SISTER SHIPS

Joan London was born in Perth, Western Australia, in 1948, and educated at the University of Western Australia. She has worked as a teacher of English as a second language and spent 1986 writing with the assistance of a New Writers' Fellowship from the Literature Board of the Australia Council. She lives in Fremantle, Western Australia, with her husband and two children.

Sister Ships

and other stories

Joan London

A KING PENGUIN
PUBLISHED BY PENGUIN BOOKS

PENGUIN BOOKS

Published by the Penguin Group
Viking Penguin Inc., 40 West 23rd Street, New York, New York 10010, U.S.A.
Penguin Books Ltd, 27 Wrights Lane, London W8 5TZ, England
Penguin Books Australia Ltd, Ringwood, Victoria, Australia
Penguin Books Canada Ltd, 2801 John Street, Markham, Ontario, Canada L3R 1B4
Penguin Books (N.Z.) Ltd, 182–190 Wairau Road, Auckland 10, New Zealand

Penguin Books Ltd, Registered Offices:
Harmondsworth, Middlesex, England

First published in Australia by Fremantle Arts Centre Press 1986
Published in Penguin Books 1988

Some of the stories in this collection first appeared in *Decade: A Selection of Western Australian Short Fiction* and *Westerly*.

Grateful acknowledgment is made for permission to reprint excerpts from the following copyrighted works:

"Do You Want to Know a Secret" by John Lennon and Paul McCartney. © 1963 by Northern Songs Ltd., London, England. All rights for U.S. & Canada controlled by Unart Music Corporation. All rights of Unart Music Corp. assigned to SBK Catalogue Partnership. All rights administered by SBK U Catalog. International copyright secured. All rights reserved. Used by permission.

"You Are My Heart's Delight" by Frank Lehar and Harry Bache Smith. © 1929 Karczag (renewed). All rights administered by Warner Bros. Music. All rights reserved. Used by permission.

"Still Crazy After All These Years" by Paul Simon. Copyright © 1974 Paul Simon. Used by permission.

"Louisiana 1927" by Randy Newman. © 1974 Warner-Tamerlane Publishing Corp. and Randy Newman. All rights reserved. Used by permission.

LIBRARY OF CONGRESS CATALOGING IN PUBLICATION DATA
London, Joan, 1948–
Sister ships and other stories.
(King Penguin)
Contents: Sister ships—First night—New Year—[etc.]
I. Title. II. Title: Sister ships.
PR9619.3.L62S57 1988 823 87-19734
ISBN 0 14 01.0571 9 (pbk.)

Printed in the United States of America by R. R. Donnelley & Sons, Harrisonburg, VA
Set in Times Roman

To
Beau and George

Acknowledgements

Sister Ships was written with the assistance of a New Writers' Fellowship from the Literature Board of the Australia Council

Some of the stories appearing in this collection first appeared in *Decade: a selection of western australian short fiction* (Fremantle Arts Centre Press) and *Westerly*. The story 'Travelling' won the 1984 Patricia Hackett Prize.

Fremantle Arts Centre Press receives financial assistance from the Western Australian Arts Council, a statutory authority of the Government of Western Australia.

Contents

Sister Ships

Sister Ships

1.

Kaye Garrett is late again. She has rushed into the cabin in her bikini and thrown her wet towel on my bunk.

'Have I got time for a ciggie?' she asks, lighting up anyway though she knows we are First Sitting. Then she gets down to work. She circles her eyes with a sort of white lipstick and dots biscuit-coloured lotion onto the compass points of her face. I take this opportunity to slip her towel onto the floor.

'I don't know why you go to all this trouble', Bar Holland calls down from the top bunk. 'The people on this ship are only interested in food and sexual intercourse.'

'Oh?' says Kaye Garrett. 'Why do you say that?' Her eyes are open very wide in the mirror but she's not looking at us. With a little black brush she is grooming the wing of her lashes. Does she know that as she does this her mouth springs open like a fish?

'Observation', Bar Holland says. I hear her yawning. 'I haven't put it to the test.'

The dinner chimes crackle over the P.A. Doors slam up and down the corridor and a great wave of people calling out and jingling keys seems to rush past our cabin. I stand up. I have been ready for ages.

Kaye rips off her bikini and reaches into the wardrobe. 'Oh Hull.' She's turning to me, she's holding my pink shirt, 'Oh Hully, would you mind, could I please . . .?'

I take a breath. I've practised this. I was going to say, in a light, pleasant voice, 'Actually Kaye, I'd thought of wearing that myself tomorrow'. But when she stands in front of me like this, naked, watching me, as if she's testing me, I don't know where to look . . .

There is a quick knock and the door swings open. Kaye screams and clutches my shirt to her.

'Sorry ladeez, so sorry ladeez.' It is Taki, our cabin steward, with an armful of towels. He backs out, groping to close the door behind him.

'Bloody Taki', Kaye says. She's buttoning up my shirt.

'Hot Greek blood', calls down Bar.

'He must have thought we'd gone to dinner', I say. 'We *are* late.' In the mornings I find him waiting outside the door with his mop and duster. I say, 'I'm sorry. The other girls are still slee-ping.' I put my head on my hands to mime a pillow. He nods and smiles. He understands.

'Oh yeah?' says Kaye. 'He's always barging in.' She's pulling on a black skirt, tucking in my shirt. The pink shirt is part of an ensemble my mother and I bought after my last day at school. 'For deck games', my mother said. Sometimes I think about the Trip as my mother planned it. It is like another ship travelling alongside this one, with all its passengers on deck waving in a friendly sort of way. There are bound to be some awfully nice types amongst them, my parents had a ball on their Trip Out, they are waving but getting hard to see now, the animal throb and grind of this ship is leaving them behind.

The lights flicker in the narrow corridors. We stagger a little as the ship sways. Voices are rising in the bars, 'Aloha' and 'Chelsea', where the early drinkers have settled in. As our heels clatter up the stairs two stewards hiss from a doorway: 'Psst! I love you!' We look straight ahead but we giggle. Don't they know that with us their case is hopeless?

We part at the doors of the dining-room. Kaye Garrett sort of glides in past us, gone for the night.

'I'll meet you here afterwards', I say to Bar Holland. If I don't say this she is quite likely to wander off in her absent-minded way, and then I am alone for the whole evening. '*Here,* okay?'

'Okay', she says. She brings her book with her. She sits at a table with a big family. Quite often they are sea-sick and only the father is there. He is glad of a bit of peace and quiet, Bar says. He's quite happy if she reads between courses.

My table is for four, on the far side of the dining-room. I take my usual seat, next to the German man. I say Good Evening to him, I have never caught his name. He wears a white suit to dinner and has a short white beard. He's about my father's age: it is his eleventh sea voyage. This is all I know about him.

'We thought you were going to miss out on the soup', Marie says from across the table. She is a secretary from Wollongong. 'Still not to worry, we've only just got ours as usual.' Marie is frustrated by the service on this ship, especially at the table. 'It's the same old story', she told me, 'the quiet ones get overlooked'.

'Hi', says Eric, who sits next to her.

'Try and catch the waiter's eye', Marie advises me, 'when he goes to that big table'.

But I don't want any soup. I am trying to think of something to say to Eric.

'How did you go at deck-tennis this afternoon?'

He laughs. 'I got a thrashing. I'm out of the tournament. I think I'm going to have to invent deck-cricket. Maybe I'd make a better fist of that.'

I laugh, understandingly. I know that Eric plays cricket in summer, swims all year round, likes early Blues and opera, grew up on a farm in northern New South Wales, has just finished his second year of Law. I know because over two weeks' meals I have asked him. The trouble is, I'm running out of questions. He asks me questions too sometimes, often the same questions. I've told him three times now that I've just done my matric, that I'm going to stay with relatives in England.

'Get a load of that would you', Marie says. 'That big table. On to the main course already and we haven't even ordered the entrée!'

'I met another girl from Perth today', Eric says to me.

His nose is sunburnt, a big nose, he isn't really good-looking. But the first time he came to our table and smiled and pulled Marie's chair out for her, I thought: He's *nice*.

'A blonde girl, Barbara.'

'Oh, Bar Holland. She went to school with me. She shares my cabin.'

'She seems like quite an original.'

'Yes. Well I didn't really get to know her before this trip. We were in different classes . . .'

'You can't have any secrets when you share a cabin, I can tell you', Marie says.

'Do you share a cabin?' I ask the German man after a while. It seems so terribly rude not to say anything to him for the whole meal.

'I am alone', the German man replies. 'I prefer.'

'I think I would too.' I give a little laugh. 'Not that I've got any secrets.'

'Ah', says the German man. 'Without secrets nothing is possible.'

'What *is* your cabin number by the way?' Eric asks me.

'There she is', I say to Bar Holland. We are taking our after-dinner stroll around A Deck.

'Who?'

'*Kaye.* It looks like it's Officers' Night tonight.'

'Chelsea' is dimly lit, but the pink shirt, the white uniforms around it, glow in the light from behind the bar.

'I suppose it's a good way to learn Greek', I say, climbing up the ladder onto Boat Deck behind Bar Holland. There is a railing at the front of Boat Deck, past the funnels, where we always stand. It is as high and far as you can go.

I want to talk about Kaye Garrett with Bar, but something holds me back. 'All that make-up', I want to say, 'do you think she looks *hard?* Do you think she looks older than seventeen? I think swearing is unfeminine. Does she swear in front of men? What is sex-appeal anyway? She's got lots of nice clothes herself, I don't know why she . . .'

It is quieter up here, we are further away from the engine, you can even hear the crisp breaking of the wake, white in the black sea. The wind blows back Bar Holland's beach-white hair from her long, stern chin. Her eyelashes are white too, so that her stare beyond the ship seems unblinking. I wish that I was like Bar Holland, my mind on higher things.

'Think I'll go down and read', she says.

'Yes', I say, 'I *must* finish my letter'.

Music has started up in the ballroom. The soft thud of the drum, the even ripple of the piano. *'Leesten',* the singer's voice crackles as he adjusts the microphone, *'do you want to know a see-gret?'*

Corridor by corridor we descend the ship.

We went to the ballroom once, on our first night aboard. Kaye was with us then. We sat at a table by the dance-floor and ordered drinks. 'To us', Kaye said. The band, in midnight-blue tuxedos, winked and bowed at us. There was a solo on the electric guitar, the theme song from 'Bonanza'. A middle-aged couple danced a professional tango under the swirling gold hexagons of the dome in the middle of the ceiling.

'Oh my God', Kaye Garrett said, 'This is *dire.*'

But after a while the ballroom filled with people, Second Sitting people. The band took off their coats. The dance floor thronged, lights dimmed, shadows raced around the walls. A white uniform bowed before Kaye. She got up slowly, her face was severe over his shoulder as they circled the floor. Bar Holland and I sipped our drinks, islanded amongst empty tables and chairs. Bar Holland stood up.

'I'm going', she said. 'I'm bored.'

We made a great show of fanning ourselves on the deck, of gasping for fresh air.

'Who do you write all these letters to?' Bar Holland's bunk creaks above me as she changes position, sighs, flicks pages. I look at my watch. 9.30. We have made our descent too early. But there's no going back. That would be against our code, our anti-ship stance. And I've already rollered up my hair.

'Oh — my parents mainly', I say.

'S'pose I ought to drop the folks a line', says Bar. 'But what do you say? "I am eating, sleeping and reading.

Fondest regards".'

'I'm sure they'd like to know how you are.'

The bunk thumps, Bar Holland's legs wave past me. She crouch-lands on the floor. 'They know I'm alive', she says. 'The rest is just — role play.'

'But your parents — well, they feel for you', I say from the shadows of my bunk.

'Do they?' She is walking up and down the cabin breast-stroking the air. 'How do you know what you feel if you just keep on spouting off your lines?' Her voice trails off, she yawns. 'Anyway', she mutters, 'I don't seem to go in for *feelings*'.

There's a knock at the door. I shrink back clutching my rollers. Bar Holland opens it an inch. Her blouse at the back is hanging out of her skirt. Her hair is fizzed into a little crown from lying down.

'Oh it's you', she says. She sounds almost angry. 'Oh all right, why not.' She reaches for her key on the dressing-table.

It's Eric.

2.

You should see me now, I write, *lying back next to the swimming pool!* I pause. This is more or less the case. It was a relief to see this empty deckchair as I picked my way through all those brown oily bodies. 'Yes dear, come and join me', the old lady in the next chair said. She's asleep now. We're not all that far from the pool. *The weather is perfect, everybody is here.* I waved to Kaye Garrett but she didn't see me. She's amongst a very lively crowd of people. Marie waves though, from under her big sunhat, while another girl rubs cream into her shoulders. Even the German man is standing by the railing, looking at something through binoculars. *Bar Holland's in the pool, having a swimming lesson!* Eric kneels by the side of the pool while Bar thrashes her way up and back to him. When she emerges, spouting water, hair plastered over her eyes, Eric leans right down to her to demonstrate a stroke.

Luckily I have the cabin to myself a lot these days. I am teaching English to our steward. He brings me his photos and I point and say 'brother-in-law', 'grandmother' etc. He is very grateful. His knock is so gentle it might be just another note in the rattle and hum of the cabin. The cool dark cabin. I shut my eyes against the white glare of the deck. *Actually it's getting very hot out here, I can't last much longer. I don't think I'm ever going to finish this letter!*

The funny thing is, I can't see my parents any more. I mean I can't see their faces. I see them as silhouettes moving round the rooms at home, dark figures against light coming through doors and windows. I see light coming onto the kitchen table, onto the knives and forks in their set places, but the room is empty. I see the pool of light under their bedroom door. Voices . . . *join in . . . people of her own age . . . the Garrett girl has got a berth . . .*

I see my father's big frame blocking the light of the hall as he comes in from checking the letter-box. The jingle of small change in his pockets has a disappointed sound.

'Do *you* speak French too?' Eric asks me at lunch.

'No.'

'That's a pity. We could have put in a bit of practice over *déjeuner.*' He is buttering his roll lavishly, smiling to himself.

'Bar Holland got the French prize at school', I say. It is Cold Cuts for lunch again today. I choose a small slice of Luncheon Meat. 'And then of course this scholarship to Paris.'

'Well she's got a real challenge on her hands now', Eric says. 'She's going to have me speaking French by the time we get to Southampton.'

'Ah ha', says the German man, his voice cracking out, crusty. We all turn to him. 'That is the best way to learn a language. The language of love.' His head shakes up and down over his plate. I can't tell if he's laughing. We all bend back over our plates.

'Bar will do it if anyone can', I say. I reach for the Worcestershire sauce and shake it over my meat. 'Not only is she terribly intelligent, she is a very hard worker.' I take my time, making a little package for my fork. 'At school she had no time for anything else. No sport, no social life. It was work work work.' The ship dips, the bright water in the porthole behind Eric flashes on, flashes off. The words keep coming. 'She was sort of famous for it.'

'My cabin mate Nan and I', Marie begins, 'we can't understand a word our steward says to us. Speaka da English *please,* I say to him . . .' I can hear Eric scraping back his chair, but Marie has caught my eye and won't let go. 'Wouldn't you think they'd try and get an English-speaking crew?'

'If you'll excuse me', Eric says.

I put down my knife and fork. I can't eat the Cold Cuts. They taste of the ship's refrigerator, they taste as if they have soaked up all the smells of the ship. The ship itself is like a giant refrigerator. If you turned it off you would smell its staleness, its collective odours from a thousand lives in cold storage.

That the knock does come, at the same time as yesterday, makes it seem like an appointment. I too have my rendezvous. I don't leave him to use his key, but open the door myself.

His eyes are waiting for me. No mop, no towels. He's not pretending this time that he has work to do. I recognise the red plastic cover of his photo album.

More photos? That cheerful teaching voice. But it helps, to get me to the bunk, turn on the little spotlight over the pillow, pat a place for him.

Seester, nephew, brudder-in-lo. It is touching to see this manly hand, black hair crawling from the cuff over the fingers, stabbing so patiently.

Very good. Pounding blood seems to fill up my eyes. I peer at stoic faces clustered up the front steps of a house. A bare twiggy tree by the balcony. I point. *Brr. Cold.*

Cold? He slides an arm around me. *You are cold?*

No no. The photo. Must be winter. His thighs nudge mine, narrow and hard, like gateposts. *When it's winter in Greece, it's summer in Aus* . . . I am falling back.

You good girl. His breath is warm in my ear. *The most good girl on the sheep.*

Best. The best girl. But I . . . But my voice is small again as he covers my face with little popping kisses. Our knees rise as the bunk creaks. He lurches on top of me and flicks his tongue wetly into my ear, kisses my neck, squeezes my breasts. All this is, I know, to be expected. He is quite systematic, in a hasty way. He seems to be in a hurry.

So this is what it's like. A full close-up of a scalp. He's heavy. My legs are flattened off the edge of the bunk. There's saliva on my chin, but my arms are pinned to the elbow. I roll my eyes and catch sight of Bar Holland's big bottle-green school bloomers slung to dry over the towel-rail. It is rather clinical, I decide, like being in a dentist's chair. The same helplessness, the same need to remind yourself there is no reason to feel embarrassed. His hand is steadily ruching up my skirt. *You should see me now . . .*

'No.' I push at his shoulder. 'Please.'

He lifts his head. 'No?'

He is up like a shot, tucking in his shirt, looking round for his photo album.

'I'm sorry. I didn't mean . . .' I have broken a rule, I know. I have *led him on.*

He smiles down at me. He shrugs.

'Leetle girl.'

He ducks for a moment at the mirror on his way out and, using two hands, smooths back his hair.

3.

We are getting into colder waters now. The swimming pool is covered with a net. There are whole decks where the wind sweeps down and the spray leaps up to startle only empty deckchairs. The sea and sky have joined forces, huge, murky and untrustworthy.

'Dirty old day', the old lady from the deckchair mutters as we pass. Her head is bandaged in a scarf as if she has the mumps. We seldom pass without a nod or comment, we fellow deck-bravers, who have taken over now the brown bodies have deserted, the blind man and his wife, the mad boy counting his steps, the Indian couple, her peacock skirts brushing against wet railings, the tired-looking father from Bar Holland's table, the German man in a black, high-shouldered coat.

Inside it's different too. The rattle and sway of the ship fighting its way seems to diminish the music and the voices. The bars are cosy and crowded, all day people huddle by salt-misted windows, shrieking as their glasses slide and slop across the tables. There is a sense of closing-in, an end coming.

I see Bar Holland and Eric everywhere. If I pop my head into the Lounge, looking for a private corner, they will be there, frowning over chess. In the Writing Room, where I might sit, but never write, they are sharing a desk, whispering. I see them emerging from the Cinema, Greek Dancing Classes, the Purser's Office. Will they think I'm spying on them? They do not see me, they are too involved in a sort of permanent private debate. Bar Holland's bumpy suitcase, her pile of dog-eared paperbacks remain untouched in the cabin. Her bunk with its virgin turned-down sheet is a still-life. She is more tousled than ever, but exercise has given a sheen to the pale planes of her chin and forehead. She wears, day and night, a big sweater of Eric's.

Now that I spend so much time out of the cabin, I see a lot. I leave the cabin early, well before breakfast. I see girls with set faces weaving their way in evening clothes up dark corridors. During one of my long mornings on the deck, I see two husbands start a fight between the funnels, with little puffs of punches, stumbling feet. One night I see Kaye Garrett bent over the railing, being sick. I recognise her by the luminous fuzz of my pale-blue angora sweater. She tucks strings of hair behind her ears and zig-zags haughtily back to the bar.

If I see a uniform coming, I have my escape routes. I know my way around the secrets of the ship. I skirt roped-off passages, fortress doors, steep metal stairways marked STRICTLY CREW ONLY. I pass clattering kitchens, doors sucked closed on blackness, tiny decks just above the water where dark men smoke and laugh.

Sometimes it's unavoidable. I have to keep walking. I drop my eyes and watch my feet pass theirs. There is always a whisper, a hiss, a laugh. Once I heard it. *Leetle girl.*

I say it over and over to myself through sucked teeth. I suppose I'm hoping that, like an orange, humiliation can be sucked dry.

One night Eric is late for dinner.

'Will I order the soup for him anyway so as not to hold us up?' Marie asks me and the German man.

'This is not like Eric', she says a little later.

We eat our soup. We order and munch away silently at our Fried Schnapper à la Saint-Germaine. We are about to tackle our Bon Fillet à l'Anglais with Ribbon Potatoes when Marie spots him. By turning in my chair and following the direction of her faintly shaking finger I can see him too, wedged in next to a pillar far across the dining-room. A fork stabs the air in front of him. A blonde head subsides behind the pillar.

'We've been deserted!' says Marie. She leans over and takes Eric's bread roll, pops it in her bag. 'Aren't I awful?' she says to me. 'Nan and I get starving after Bingo.'

Like Marie and the German man I eat steadily, right through to the Sherry Trifle and Selected Cheeses, and leave my plate bare.

When the P.A. announces that at twenty-one hours and ten minutes precisely we will be passing our Sister Ship, I climb the ladder to the old place on Boat Deck. The sky is star-dazzled. Nobody else seems to be around.

A row of lights comes suddenly out of darkness and rushes towards us. I can feel our own pace now as the Sister Ship takes shape, slides her long glittering flank beside us. The two ships snort at one another like animals from the same litter, mournful bellows across the frothing wakes. Rockets spray out from between the answering sets of funnels. I glimpse long shelves of decks under swinging lights, hear scraps of frantic music. Tiny figures lift their hands: I have lifted mine, like a salute. Then they are gone.

I sleep a great deal. I dream. I dream I am sitting at the table with Marie and the German man. The waiter puts before me a big plate of bones. Large, angular bones, freshly butchered, tufted with meat and cold white fat. I am unable to stop myself attacking the bones. I gnaw, dribble and crunch: as I throw one over my shoulder I reach for another. I shut my eyes and groan with satisfaction. Marie and the German man watch me. Marie shakes her head, sorrowful. 'You are very greedy', she says.

One morning the wild black decks are forbidden to the passengers. But it's the dangerous hour below, when stewards come out with sheets and keys. I slip through Reading Rooms, Cocktail Lounges, the deserted bars. I come to the ballroom. On the stage the piano is open and the German man is playing. I take a seat at one of the empty tables across the floor.

At first I watch the German man. He has gathered his long private face together as if he is regretful about something. He makes mistakes, stumbles, only just makes it over a hill of notes, but he never stops, his fingers push on, bite down.

Then I pick up a pattern in the notes. Just as I wait for it again it breaks up, scatters, comes together differently. It seems to me the music has a voice that knows more than I ever will, that leads me on, further, further, and at the last minute shows me where it is the pattern really lies.

The German man throws his hands into his lap and swivels on his stool. He shows no surprise at seeing me.

'I play very badly', he says, shaking his head, though to me he seems flushed and exhilarated. 'I do not practise for a long time.'

'I wish I could play like that.'

'The Hammierclavier. First and second movements.' He gets out a handkerchief and slowly wipes his face. 'It is just like anything else. At first it is technical and then the meaning starts to come as you learn the piece.'

As I get up to go he says, 'You should hear it played — right — one day'.

'Yes, I will try', I say.

'I've put on that much weight', Marie sighs over soup. 'Still not to worry, I'll probably have to starve in London.'

Our destination is very close now. Suitcases block the corridors. There are flustered queues outside the Purser's Office. Addresses are exchanged in bars rowdy with farewell. The waiters slap down our plates. The menus are stained and repetitive. I take two sips of my Creme Milanese, crumble my roll.

'You're not pregnant are you?' Marie says with a wink at the German man. 'I bet you wouldn't be the only one.'

The German man eats on as if he hasn't heard.

'The trouble with you is', she says a little later, leaning over to me, 'you're a worrier. You mightn't think it, but I'm a worrier too.'

I have noticed that lines spray out from Marie's eyes and mouth and tendons strain in her neck when she peers at other tables.

'That's why I'm on this trip. You've got to get out of yourself, mix in.'

I don't dare look at the German man.

'I tell you what', Marie goes on, 'Nan and I are going to the Fancy Dress Ball tonight. It's the farewell do. Why don't you come along, make it a three?'

'I will think up a cozzie for us', she says with a wink. 'Leave it to me.'

'Tonight at eight-thirty then, my cabin', she says.

The German man looks at his watch, stands up, nods to us.

'I'll be glad to see the end of him', Marie says, as we watch his square white back leave the dining-room. 'There's something about him . . . you know?'

She reaches over and takes his orange.

Kaye Garrett is sitting cross-legged on her bunk, writing. I have not seen her for days. I ask her if she's going to the Fancy Dress Ball.

'You've got to be joking.'

She doesn't look as if she's going anywhere. She is wearing just a T-shirt, bending through her bare knees to an exercise book and ashtray on the coverlet.

I sit down on my bunk. 'What are you writing?'

'My diary.' She doesn't stop. Her hair is scraped back into a pony-tail. She is left-handed. She writes very fast, her hand looping like a child's.

After a while she looks up. Her face is scrubbed of make-up, her skin looks damp and porous, there are dark circles under her eyes. This is how she used to look, last year. Her house was right near the school, by the river. She would stalk into the classroom late, breathing morning steam. While she stuffed her beret into her pocket, her eyes travelled the desks, as if she was counting something up. Or looking for something.

'I'm trying to sort out where I stand', she says. 'I'm in the shit all over the ship. Greek men are terribly possessive Hull.'

She bends to write. I can just hear the scratch of her pen. It has a companionable sound.

'Maybe I won't go to that ball', I say.

'You've got to do what you want *I* think.'

She is still writing when I get up to go.

'Bye Hully', she says, quite gently.

It is strange to leave Kaye Garrett behind me. Through the corridors I think of her bent head against the shadows of the cabin, and the scratch of her pen, writing.

I can hear the rustling even as I knock on Marie's door.

'Oh there you are', she says, pulling me inside. She is wrapped neck to foot in white crepe paper. 'Put your arms up! Come on! We're going to miss the Grand Parade.' She starts to wind white paper around me too, so that we both crackle like bonfires. 'Pins Nan!' she calls. 'This is the little lass I've been telling you about, the one from Perth.'

Nan is not in costume. I recognise her as the girl who's often with Marie, the one with the long neck and the red-rimmed eyes as if she's just been crying. She smiles at me through little childish teeth.

'Don't move', Marie hisses through pins.

'What are we?'

'Guess!' She waves two cylinders of black crepe paper at me. Each has an uneven white cross glued to it. 'Our crowning glory', she says, 'Oh what a hoot!'

Nan wedges one onto my head while Marie adjusts hers in the mirror. They press down over our eyebrows. We look at one another with pained, spaniel-hooded eyes.

'Sister Ships', says Marie. 'These are our Funnels. Aren't I clever?'

She slings a whistle on a string around my neck. 'Your foghorn. The idea is, in the Grand Parade we sort of run past each other blowing our whistles.'

'Come on', she says, looking at my face, 'don't go and chicken out on me like Nan. It's only for laughs. You can reimburse me for the paper and pins etc tomorrow.'

We totter up the stairs. The wind catches us as we cross the deck to the ballroom and we rustle like an army of bats. We clutch our funnels. 'They're going to die when they see us', Marie whispers.

We enter the ballroom to a burst of cheering and wolf-whistles. But the crowd has their backs to us. As we crane, funnels lurching, the band strikes up, the lights dim, the crowd moves off onto the floor. Marie does not waste time on regrets.

'Now is our chance', she says over her shoulder, swerving a course through dancing couples. She piles bags and coats onto a vacated table, drags the chairs right to the edge of the floor.

'Excuse me, excuse me', she says, pulling a third chair from under a flailing hand, and sitting down on it.

'I learnt the hard way on this ship believe me', she says, as Nan and I slide down next to her. 'Nobody's going to lift a finger for you.' She hails a waiter. 'What'll be your pleasure, girls? Going to join me in an Athens' Special?'

I am glad Marie is not too disappointed about missing the Grand Parade. She seems to be thoroughly enjoying herself, peering at the costumes as they pass on the dance floor. There are a lot of men dressed up as women, even pregnant women, with signs like SUZY WENT WONG and I SHOULD HAVE DANCED ALL NIGHT pinned on their backs. 'Oh get a load of this one', Marie cries, slapping my knee. It is a man in a nightie and a necklace of gin bottles. He is called OFFICERS MESS. 'Oh there'll be some red faces here tonight.' She has to wipe her eyes.

The band launches into 'I Did It My Way'. For this the lead singer undoes the buttons of his shirt. It is very hot and stuffy. We have drunk our Athens' Specials. Marie sends Nan off to get some more.

An Arab headdress bows before me.

'Go on', Marie nudges me. 'It's Dennis from Bingo.'

Dennis and I sway together for a while with linked, clammy hands.

'The band is very *thing* tonight isn't it?' he says.

'Yes.' I can't see his face, he's wearing dark glasses, like a sheikh.

'I got this Arab outfit in Aden. What are you supposed to be? Nurses? The Ku Klux Klan?'

'Sister Ships.'

'What?' The band is very loud.

'Sister Ships.'

'Oh ha ha, well don't let it worry you', he says. I don't think he can hear me. He takes me back to my seat and asks Nan to dance. As they bump past I hear him say to her, 'The band is very *thing* tonight isn't it?'

The band plays 'The Girl From Ipanema' and people start to clap and move to the edge of the dance floor. Marie and I sip our drinks and peer through the crowd. The professional dance couple are at it again, under the swirling gold dome. Up and down they pass one another, back and forward, flashing smiles over their shoulders, they turn at the same moment, up and down again, it's a sort of prowl, back and forward . . . it makes me dizzy.

I blink and blink at the couple and it is suddenly clear to me that they are my parents. They are in disguise of course, like all of us: they have been on board all the time! It's their movements that give them away. The way they hold their backs so straight and know their steps so well, everything's planned . . . though there's something rather fixed about their smiles, they're not quite real, the way their arms flare out from the elbow at the same time reminds me of puppets . . .

'Your shout', Marie is saying, pushing her glass at me. Her funnel has slipped over one eye.

I stand up with the glasses, keeping an eye on my parents. I edge around the dance floor towards the bar. It is very important that they don't see me. I'm afraid that if they did they might call out to me, make me join in. I have come this far without them now.

The ship lurches. I have to watch my steps very carefully, but I keep the gold dome swirling in the corner of my eye.

I look up and I see him. The German man, standing by the ballroom door. He is wearing not only his white suit, but also white gloves with which he holds his drink. On his head are fixed two large white ears.

I come and stand before him.

He bows. I see that his ears are two ship serviettes, like the ones that sit on our table, stiff white cones pulled into peaks. I glimpse the thin wire to which they are attached, circling his head.

The ship lurches the other way. He puts down his drink. He inclines his head very slightly towards the door.

'Ready?' he says. I could swear his ears twitch.

I am rustling down a long corridor. My funnel has fallen off, my crepe paper rips and drags behind me.

I am sure I saw something white flash around that corner.

First Night

'I see it in sort of Greek letters', said Jonelle. 'You know, like bent branches.'

'In red ink', said Virginia. As usual she had missed the point.

'No, pink', said Amanda. 'Pink ink, pink ink.'

Antonia ignored them all. She stared a moment longer at the sheet of thick white paper spread out on her bedroom floor. Then, her mouth held as if she were about to say something thoughtful, rocking on her heels between paintbox and paper, she began.

THE PORTER STREET PLAYERS

'Proudly present . . .', said Jonelle. She had planned the alliteration weeks ago.

PROUDLY PRESENT

Antonia's brush seemed to slash the paper. Each letter was born swift and straight, with a sibling resemblance to its neighbour, a gravy thickness at their crowns, a taper to each tail . . .

ALICE AT THE BALL

'That's good Ant', said Virginia.

THE CAST
IN ORDER OF APPEARANCE

They had decided to be democratic.

AMANDA DE WITT

'Are you putting in our roles?' Jonelle asked.
'There are too many', said Antonia.

ANTONIA DE WITT
JONELLE HUGHES
VIRGINIA DE WITT

'Put our ages in, Ant', said Amanda. 'You know, Antonia de Witt — 12, Virginia De Witt — 10 . . .'

'What have ages got to do with anything?' Jonelle asked her.

'Then everybody'll know that I'm only seven and a half if I make a mistake.' Amanda looked up through her fringe.

'You won't *make* any mistakes', Jonelle said.

PERFORMANCE COMMENCES AT 8PM SHARP

Antonia sat back to look at her work, head on one side. Far away, down the long cool halls of the De Witt's house, you could hear the vacuum cleaner. Jonelle had glimpsed Mrs De Witt in the lounge-room on her way to Antonia's room for the dress-rehearsal this morning. *Like a whirlwind,* that was what Jonelle thought when she saw Mrs De Witt doing the housework, bent over the vacuum stalk, kicking furniture out of the way with her bandy brown legs in their tiny bright white shorts, not looking up or speaking to anyone. She hated housework, Antonia said, she was used to having servants. But she vacuumed like this every day, and by lunch-time she would be sunbathing in the back garden in her bikini.

Now Antonia picked up two clean brushes, dipped them in pink, in green. Barely holding the brushes, barely touching the paper, she sent a spray of pink and green lines out from the words of the title. There was silence in the bedroom except for the tinkle of Antonia's brush in water. The telephone rang. The vacuum cleaner stopped. The telephone was silenced. Outside the crickets chipped away at the long patient days of the holidays. Antonia's brushes worked and swirled in the paintbox compartments like frantic little animals muddying themselves.

Antonia straightened up. They all stood looking down at the poster. The pink and green lines shot out from behind the words like fireworks. *Their names in lights.*

'That looks really good', Jonelle said. If she had spent days and days on the poster, it would have looked . . . home-made. 'It's so professional.' She and Antonia liked that word.

'It's super', Amanda said. All the De Witts said 'super'.

'You think so?' Antonia stooped before the mirror of her dressing-table for a moment, and exchanged an enquiring look with herself, half-profile. She pushed up the sleeves of her apricot-coloured shirt. They had bought it in Mauritius on their way to Australia. Antonia called it her 'chemise'.

'Let's hang it up', said Virginia.

Antonia flapped the poster casually, to dry.

'Keep *away',* she said as her sisters danced around her down the hall. The poster was to hang on the folding door of the De Witt's dining-room where tonight's performance would take place.

'Then we'd better get on with the rehearsal', Jonelle called after them. She started to sort out the costumes that lay around the room. In order of appearance. First Amanda's Alice costume, for the Prologue. *'Hello, it's me again',* Jonelle chanted into the mirror for a moment. *'You know, I found it hard to settle back into ordinary life after Wonderland. Everything seemed so dull.'* (She takes up her book of fairytales. Yawns.) *'Ho hum, I think I'll just sit down over here and read my book. Where was I? Oh yes — "Cinderella". Oh, I'm so sleepy. Nothing ever happens any more . . .'* (Yawns again.)

There was a blue light in Antonia's room, from the sun behind the blue net curtains. In her mirror, your face was shadowed, significant. You couldn't see your freckles, or the shallow grey-ish colour of your eyes, Australian eyes. If you moved in a bit closer and looked serious, you could almost see how you might look, one day in the future . . .

After Alice falls asleep, to the strains of 'Les Sylphides' on the De Witts' portable (they'd have to practice putting the needle down so it didn't scratch), there was Antonia's Cinderella scene. For this she wore — where was it? The pink cotton dress, late of Judith Hughes, too faded to hand on to Jonelle. It hung in becoming waif-like folds on Antonia. The Hughes were altogether a bigger breed than the De Witts. That was why Jonelle was the Prince, and the Stepmother and the White Rabbit's Tail.

'All by myself again,
Here by the fire . . .'

Jonelle sang Cinderella's song softly as she worked. This was luxury, like gloating over your collected birthday presents. The way the costumes interwove like the play did, threaded through with strokes of luck and genius . . . waking at night with the thought 'Alice *is* the Fairy Godmother' clear in her head, shouting 'I've got it!' across the fence to Antonia, 'See, they all talk in rhyme except for Alice!' . . . Limp things now, like the costumes, waiting to come to life again, tonight. To glow out of darkness, like the little theatre in her head. *The audience rose to its feet . . . There were cries of 'author, author'. Blinking modestly in the footlights . . .*

Down the hall there was a collision of voices, high-pitched De Witt voices, exaggerating their clipped sing-song.

'Out of the question!' called out Mrs De Witt.

A door slammed. Antonia came running into the room and cast herself over the bed, costumes and all. She groaned loudly and beat her pillow. Virginia and Amanda hovered at the door.

'Mummy says we're not to use the dining-room table on any account', Virginia whispered to Jonelle. A half-smile flickered on her face.

'Mummy's a bitch', said Antonia, turning her staring eyes onto them for a moment. 'The play is off.' She put the pillow over her head.

'What's the matter love?' Mrs Hughes had wandered into Jonelle's room. She was eating a sandwich, carrying a plate, for the crumbs, across her chest.

'Mm', she said between bites. 'I didn't get around to breakfast this morning.' The bed creaked as she sat down.

Jonelle kept her face turned to the wall. Lately she hadn't been able to look at her mother when she was eating. It made her sad or sick or something. The way her mouth moved so quickly, like a little beak . . .

'Why the long face?'

'Oh Antonia's thrown another maddie and the whole play's off.'

Mrs Hughes picked up her second sandwich. 'My word, she's a highly-strung little lass.'

Jonelle turned onto her stomach.

'Never mind. I expect you're just worn out with all this play-acting. Why don't you have a little sleep and then a bite of . . .'

'No', said Jonelle. 'I don't want a little sleep.' These days her mother was always saying that Jonelle was outgrowing her strength. There she went again, pulling down the blind, closing the door softly after her, like she did when Jonelle was sick.

She could never tell her mother anything.

For a start, you could never get her support. 'Do unto others', said Molly with a warning eye across the kitchen, if you started to say that you hated someone, who was mean or ugly or boring. She had heard her mother say that Jonelle now had some nice little friends next door. Nice little friends. How to explain to her. Their difference.

For instance, at the beach the other day. 'Going bathing', they called it.

'Ooh look Moggie', Mrs De Witt said to Amanda (they all had these family nick-names), 'look at the fat lady trying to swim!'

The De Witts hooted and squealed as the Fat Lady lay back in the shallows and supported her giant body with little paddling movements of her hands. Her bathing-cap bobbed bravely . . .

'Fat people get hot too', Jonelle muttered.

'If you let yourself look like that', Antonia said firmly, 'you shouldn't parade it'.

No good trying to tell her mother. There are fat ladies. *Fat.* And people laugh at them.

If you half-shut your eyes, there was a neon frame around the window where the blinds held back the sun. It was getting hot in her room. Jonelle hung her arm over the edge of the bed and ran the back of her fingers along the lino. As she used to run her hand in water, from the boat, at Rockingham, when they went on fishing holidays long ago. She could see it like an old photo — Molly Hughes wears a yellowed school panama tied under her chin with a scarf, in a bonnet effect. Also an old shirt of her husbands, to protect her speckled arms from the sun. The rest of them wear squashed cloth hats and zinc-white noses. Arthur Hughes stares intently at a distant shoreline, waiting for a bite. He chews at something small and invisible at the front of his mouth. When he lands a fish though, and chases the little blighter flapping on the floor of the boat, he snorts with half-exclamations — 'By Jing . . . What the . . .', and you can see that it's all right, he's happy, he's forgotten the office. Judith too is a keen fisherwoman. She sits over the line with her chin jutting, as if she is listening for something. She has taken off her hat because Molly says the sun is good for teenage skin problems. She and Arthur make a business-like team, baiting hooks and untangling lines for Molly and Jonelle.

'Yew — are my heart's desire'

sings Molly in the quavering mothball voice Jonelle loves.

'And where yew are
I want to be-ee.'

'Sea-water runs in my veins', she sighs, wedged up in the bows of the boat. She rummages under the seat for one of her lunches, a thermos of tea, warm cordial for the girls, tomato sandwiches, pink, in greaseproof, and a bit of left-over Christmas cake. When she tries to hand Arthur his tea, the boat rocks wildly, Molly halloos and tips backwards, in fits.

'Mu-um', says Judith. 'You'll scare off the fish.'

Even Arthur is smiling. 'We need you for ballast dear', he says, 'so do us a favour, stay in the bows'. He gives one of his short barks, so rare you want to join in loudly to encourage him.

The boat bobs on the sheeny water, Molly sings, the poor fish thump for help in their hessian bag. 'I suppose you're sorry for them', Judith says over her shoulder. Jonelle has given up on fishing, trails her hand in water, across her own reflection. Nothing can touch them on that boat, no one can see them, they can bob, bob, bob like this forever, the Hughes family afloat.

There was another, more private picture from that lost time, pre-De Witt. Jonelle's back disappearing behind the hibiscus at the end of the yard. No more photos allowed. Private. Keep out. Not that there was anything to see. Mutters, frowns, pacings between the incinerator and the compost heap. Stories, set to action. Words. *'The ragged girl shivered and looked for wild berries before she set off across the moors.'* Or 'the mountains' or 'the snow'. The Northern Hemisphere. Nothing inspiring ever happened in Australia.

An intensely private activity, this. Jonelle called it 'going up the back'. If anyone should come, her father with his wheelbarrow for instance, she would hum and pretend to be looking for something in the shed. Though the intrusion too could be used. Her father would never know as he emptied his grass-clippings, that he was a Nazi guard in a series you could loosely call 'Anne Frank Strikes Back', and that it was because of him that Jonelle was inching her way along the back fence, across the roofs of Amsterdam.

Since the De Witts had come, Jonelle had stopped going up the back. She had tried it once or twice, but it hadn't worked.

When the De Witts had first moved into MacDougalls' place next door, Jonelle, no great lover of tennis, had practised her fore-hand against the garage door one evening after tea. After a while, prodding one another in the back, the two younger girls, the ones with the blonde plaits and the spindly white legs and those funny buckled-up sandals that English kids always wore, came over and stood watching her.

'How old are you?' Amanda asked her.

'Twelve', said Jonelle, swiping at her ball.

'My sister Antonia is twelve', said Amanda.

'She's a duffer at ball-games', said Virginia. Their voices were straight out of Enid Blyton. Did they go blackberrying in the hols, ride donkeys at the seaside, explore ruined Abbeys?

'She has a beautiful singing voice', said Amanda. 'She's going to be an actress. She can also draw and write poetry.'

'Our father bought her a typewriter', said Virginia. 'He's going to buy me a tennis racquet for my birthday.'

Jonelle offered her a turn with the ball.

'Virginia! Amanda! Come here please.' The older sister was calling, like a parent, from the porch of the great white slab of their house, the biggest house in Porter Street. All around the porch was wrought iron, painted black. Jonelle had long fancied that porch for a balcony scene, something set in Spain.

Amanda ran over to her sister. She brought her back, holding her by the hand.

'This is Antonia', she said to Jonelle.

Antonia was very slight and white, like her sisters. But she had wide-spun reddish-brown hair and dark eyes set at the corners of her small triangular face. She was almost very pretty. She did not look friendly.

'Are you like Virginia?' she said to Jonelle. 'Very *sportive?*'

'Not really', said Jonelle. She was conscious that her shorts belled out from her crutch, and that her feet, which by this time of the year were tough enough to walk across the road at midday, were splayed and grey with dirt.

'What *do* you like to do?'

'Well', said Jonelle. An idea shot up her spine, into her head *sideways,* like the best ideas, complete. 'I make things up', she said, as the bright darkness of the summer night fell around them. 'Plays and things.' They were like something out of a book, these girls, and she too had her lines to say. It was as if she held them all, and the summer ahead of them, in her hand like a book.

'I'm doing *Little Women* at the moment', she said,

looking around at them. Meg, Jo, Beth and Amy. She would be Jo of course.

Antonia was watching her with her head to one side. 'Would you like to come to our house', she said, 'and have a drink or something?'

The De Witts had drinks on their back terrace every evening when Mr De Witt came home from work. They had always done this, Antonia said, in Africa, in Saudi Arabia, in Indonesia, everywhere that the Company had sent them.

'Daddy, make her stay!' Antonia would call out if Jonelle tried to edge her way towards the fence. So Mr De Witt would hand her a glass of lemonade with a little bow, and Jonelle would crouch down on the terrace steps next to Antonia, and try to drink the lemonade without gulping. Something about Mr De Witt made her shy.

'How are my actresses today?' What she guarded like a mute from her family was pass-the-salt chit-chat for the De Witts. It made her queasily excited.

Mr De Witt seemed to know everything about his daughters. He sat on the big stone barbecue, legs dangling, guarding his drink between his knees from his younger daughters as they swarmed around him. His legs were dainty, not like a man's, small curved calves, trim little ankles, high insteps . . . what would he think if he knew how much Jonelle knew about him? Antonia had talked for hours about her father, in a low voice late in the afternoons. They walked up and down Porter Street or lolled on Antonia's bed. She called him 'Witti' in these stories. Everyone called him that. Witti's brilliant career as a student at Witwatersrand University. His scholarship to Oxford. Heresies. He was an atheist. A pacifist.

When Mrs De Witt had accepted his proposal of marriage, two days after he had met her in the British Museum, he had *cried.* Once Mrs De Witt had packed all the girls into a plane in Indonesia and flown back to London because of somebody called Aunty Pearl.

'You mean — he fell in love with her?'

Antonia turned her palm up, then down. 'Maybe. She

was very beautiful. She was half a princess. They didn't think I was old enough to understand but I knew everything.'

Was that why Mrs De Witt was always so unsmiling, lying back in the cane lounge in her unmotherly shorts, smoking a cigarette? Had she forgiven him? She looked relaxed at any rate, her short blonde hair was fluffed out and she had put on some orange lipstick. You could never see what she was thinking behind her glasses, round wire spectacles, the sort that spinsters and librarians were supposed to wear, glinting now in the sun which was still high over the garden.

Still, there was Witti, family man, struggling to sip his drink as Virginia and Amanda attacked him. They tickled his back, covered his eyes with their hands, swung on his legs.

'Antonia, save me!' He dashed across the terrace and hung over Antonia. Jonelle tittered to be polite, and show she knew it was just a game. For a moment his face, which she had thought to be a masculine, red-cast replica of Antonia's, filled their vision, panting and grinning. You could see his wet rough tongue, the hairs in his nose, the reddish tints in his brown eyes. Antonia pushed him away.

'Oh cold woman, Antonia!' He staggered back, hand on heart.

'Ant-arctic', said Virginia.

'Ant-agonistic', said Mrs De Witt, with a sudden little snort from her chair.

Antonia ran inside. They heard the slam of her bedroom door.

'Leave her Witti', Mrs De Witt murmured. But Witti was already at the back door, frowning, his hand in a Stop sign to the rest of them as he prepared to follow Antonia.

'Thank-you-very-much-for-the-drink', said Jonelle, unheard, ducking off towards the fence.

'What do you think of Antonia?' Jonelle had asked Judith that night as they did the dishes after tea. In the lounge-room their father and Judith's boyfriend, Dean, had given up on making conversation and turned on the News.

‘She’s all right.’ Judith was wearing one of Molly’s aprons and her outline at the sink was almost matronly. (‘Please God’, Jonelle prayed nightly, ‘don’t let me have big bosoms like Mum and Judith’. A bustline like that, which had struck Judith overnight, seemed to weigh you down, mark you like a destiny. So far, for once, He seemed to have been listening. Almost too well . . .)

‘Do you know what Antonia said?’ Jonelle went on, after a moment’s debate with herself. Since Judith had gone to business college, and met Dean — like her a member of the Church — she had become milder, sort of tamed. Her real nature, which Jonelle knew to be witheringly down-to-earth, was covered over now with a determined charity. She had to be pushed a bit. ‘She said: *“Your sister’s seventeen. Why doesn’t she wear make-up?”*’

‘Oh did she?’ Judith sloshed dishes onto Jonelle’s side. ‘She’s got a nerve . . .’ She was still for a moment. ‘Actually, I reckon she’s a bit put-on.’

‘Mm.’ Jonelle went silent. The little stab of sly gratification felt shabby now. Judas. Whichever side she went on seemed to bring her to this point. To betray.

Like the time she and Antonia had gone to town to see the matinee of ‘Song Without End’ with Dirk Bogarde. It was terribly moving and sad. Afterwards they had stood on the Terrace waiting for their bus, hardly knowing where they were. This could happen when you got talking to Antonia.

‘And then the way he just *looked* at her when she was leaving’, said Jonelle.

‘Like this’, said Antonia. She lifted one eyebrow and slowly shook her head, Dirk Bogarde on the Terrace.

‘That’s it, do it again Ant!’

‘I can do it because I understand him, he’s my sort of man.’

‘Mm. I would never have left him . . .’

‘There’s something to be said for great exits . . .’

‘But what about going on, inspiring one another, having children . . .’

‘I will never have children’, said Antonia. ‘It spoils the figure.’

Just then Jonelle saw two girls from her class at school, walking straight towards her. Too late to duck behind Antonia — they were waving. For some reason the sight of them filled her with panic. Beverley Hall and Jocelyn Carter. Known as Bev and Jossie. Sort of class leaders, they always joined in, got picked. Not particularly pretty or clever, but normal, so normal they had to be right. They lived on a different plane of prestige from Jonelle at school. Like parents or teachers, you mustn't disturb them, let them know what you were really like, set off their disapproval.

'Hi', called out Beverley. They stood in front of Jonelle and Antonia. You giggled from a sort of reflex action as you looked one another up and down. Like Jonelle they wore pastel dresses and shiny brown stockings and white boat-shaped shoes with fledgling heels. You could see kink marks in Jocelyn's hair from rollers.

'We've been in town all day', said Beverley. 'We're *exhausted.'*

'This is Antonia', said Jonelle. 'She lives next door.'

'How do you do', said Antonia, in a deep voice.

'Are you English or something?' asked Jocelyn. Jonelle suddenly realised how different Antonia must seem, with her red lipstick, and the Zulu beads slung around the neck of her chemise.

'Half South African and half Anglo-Russian, actually', said Antonia.

'Oh Lord', said Beverley. 'There's our bus!' They ran off down the Terrace, tripping over their heels, giggling. As they climbed aboard, Jonelle saw they were still laughing, looking over their shoulders at her and Antonia. Jocelyn said something behind her hand. It was a relief to see their bus pull out into the traffic. Thank God for the holidays. She turned to Antonia.

'What *Australian* faces those girls have', Antonia was saying, almost dreamily.

'What do you mean?'

Antonia shut her eyes. 'Big chins, brownish hair, giggles. Strong bodies. Like boys dressed up.'

Queer how you could feel the prick of loyalty, as if you

were responsible for your whole race.

Everything was absolutely still outside, midday-still, or past midday. The bedroom door slid open.

'Jonelle?' Her mother was whispering. 'You awake? Phone for you lovey.'

It was Antonia. Ringing up, with breathtaking extravagance , from next door.

'It's all settled.' Her voice was low and urgent. 'I phoned up Daddy at the Company. He spoke to Mummy. We can use the table if we keep it covered with a rug. So can you please come back right now?'

The De Witts' doorbell rang again and again, each time another guest arrived. It seemed unreal, that make-believe had the power to summon the outside world. In the dressing-room they, the Porter Street Players seemed unreal. Dream-like, Jonelle and Antonia daubed the upturned faces of Virginia and Amanda into masks like their own. Antonia's room was filled with the sweetish motherly smell of spilled powder. There was a soft knock at the door.

'Last call ladies', said Mr De Witt, drink in hand, winking. Antonia shut her eyes for a moment and then ducked to the mirror.

Rustling costumes down the corridor. Subsiding coughs and trills as the audience settled onto the rows of chairs they had arranged that afternoon in the De Witts' living-room. Then silence. One voice started up, Amanda's brave sing-song. *'Hello, it's me again'*. The words unfolded obediently out of a former existence.

Plunging onto the stage, it was true, the same deep breath as before a dive, into an underwater world, bright yet muted, the sounds and signals coming from a long way away. The words were the life-line.

> *'Cinderella! What is the meaning of this?*
> *When I kindly took you under my wing,*
> *I did not mean you to dance and sing*
> *All day.'*

The voice came out by itself, she hardly recognised it, young and scratchy.

It was lonely on stage. Antonia's eyes stared at you but didn't see you, waiting for her cue. And she seemed to be moving in slow motion, as if there was a meaning in everything she did. Even when she wasn't talking, her mouth was held carefully, to herself. Except for the red streak climbing up her neck, which she got when she was upset about something, Antonia wasn't there, acting with you. She had passed you over for the audience.

And then you got used to it. It became the air you breathed. You could even dare to look at the audience. Who laughed at all their jokes, more than they had ever hoped, and clapped them off the stage, and 'aahed' for little Alice and Cinderella in her ball-gown. Witti was their cheer-leader. You could see him at the front, his eyes and teeth gleaming. Funny the feeling that everything you said was for him. And way at the back, the familiar planes of her own parents' faces, naked-looking, their smiles subdued. Probably not wanting to show their pride. Judith was sitting in front of Dean's shoulder, shadowed by the hall light. Eyes faintly squinting. No smile. *Don't show off.* Watching for it.

It went so fast. No time to stop and play it again. They ran up and down the corridor in costume changes, nudging one another, longing to get back to that high bright place again.

'And so we say — goodn-i-ght!'

they sang, reckless and airy now, red-cheeked, the play behind them, complete, perfect.

The audience rose to their feet, clapping, but also heading for the cool of the terrace where the De Witts were serving drinks. Antonia rushed to her room. It was over. It was gone.

'Well, what do you say', said Mr De Witt, 'haven't we clever daughters?' He paused for a moment with his tray by the barbecue where Jonelle and her parents were standing.

'We were just saying, weren't we Arthur', said Molly,

'that it was a pleasure to have some nice light entertainment for a change'. Jonelle noticed that her mother was clutching and unclutching the clean hanky she always carried on social occasions. When she had come out onto the terrace and seen her parents like this, side by side, stiff, somehow irrelevant, she had realised something for the first time. Her parents were *shy*.

'Another shandy Molly?' asked Mr De Witt. 'How's your beer Arthur?'

'I'll be right thanks — er — Witti.' Jonelle had heard her father say that it was a funny sort of a name for a bloke.

'No thanks Witti', said Molly. 'But I will have one of Lydia's savouries. They look lovely. Isn't she clever?' Her hand hovered boldly over the tiny tarts on his tray. She selected, took a bite, rolled her eyes and popped the rest into her mouth, dabbing her lipstick with her hanky.

Witti moved on.

Jonelle looked round. The De Witts' friends stood about in loose impenetrable circles. All the men worked for the Company. They and their wives all smoked and laughed and talked loudly in English and other foreign accents. At Christmas they had given the De Witt girls expensive boxes of chocolates and bottles of perfume.

What was going to happen next? Something had to happen. Where was Antonia? She could only see Virginia and Amanda ducking in and out of groups, still in their costumes, carrying bowls of olives and smiling up for admiration.

'Make way for the star of the show!' someone called out behind Jonelle. She turned and saw a group parting to accept Antonia, who was steered by her father with his arm around her shoulder.

'Look who I found!' Witti said. Antonia had got changed and taken off her stage make-up. She had brushed her hair and put on lipstick.

'Where's the champagne?' someone else called out. Witti threw back his head, laughing. It was the biggest and jolliest group on the terrace. Even Lydia De Witt looked pleased.

'Tell me', said a tall tanned man, bending low over

Antonia. 'When are you going to publish your play?'

'Oh we never wrote a script or anything', Antonia said. She sounded very clipped and serious. 'We just practised a great deal until we knew the lines. My sisters are so very young you see.'

'Quite', said the man, nodding. He kept on nodding, looking at Antonia. Antonia smiled at him and looked away.

'Oh-oh-*dear'*, said Molly on the end rush of a yawn. A tiny tear escaped one eye. She smiled at Jonelle. 'You must be tired', she said.

'I'm not.'

But Arthur Hughes was already tapping Witti on the shoulder.

'We'll be off then Witti. The ladies need their beauty sleep.'

'You and I, Arthur', said Witti, half turning out of his circle, 'we'll have to stick together with all these women around us eh?'

Behind the adults' laughter Antonia mouthed 'Goodbye'.

'Friendly sort of bloke, Witti', Arthur said as the Hughes crossed the dark lawn to their own house.

'It was a lovely evening all round', said Molly. She always liked to sum up an occasion, its good points. 'Isn't that little Amanda sweet! Remembering all those lines! And Antonia really is a first-class little actress. The way she moves!'

'*I* made the play up mostly', Jonelle said into the darkness. 'It was all my idea.' She was aware of giving something up as she spoke, giving something away.

'Did you dear?' said her mother. 'Well you all did a very good job.'

In their bedroom her parents were making their bed-time noises. Creak of wardrobe doors, click of bedside lamps, pop-pop-pop of corset hooks. Little sighs and groans. Thump *thump* as her father's shoes were stowed beneath the bed. Twang of the bedsprings. A murmur. A cry as Molly spies a mosquito. *Slap.* Silence.

Jonelle tiptoed past their door. Before long they always

fell asleep like this, propped up on their pillows, their light still on, their old faces sunken into their chins, library books against their chests, their hands draped across the bedcovers as delicately as ballet dancers.

Once this bed, its creaks and sighs, its warm mountainous bodies had been a ship of safety in the night. Jonelle tiptoed on, eased open the laundry door. Outside, into the night. Up the back.

Up the back. Sand between the toes. The incinerator *ghostly in the moonlight. 'The homeless girl shivered . . .'* No, not *that*. This was real. Real things were at last happening to her.

The party was winding down at the De Witts'. If you climbed up like this onto the shed roof and eased yourself along the fence, you could see their terrace light flickering in the shadows of the trees. A few last voices, tinkles, laughs, Witti's loudest. If she wantd to, she could creep down their side of the fence, crouch behind bushes, *spy* on them . . .

There was a wail, 'Antonia!' down on the terrace. Amanda.

'I did not', she heard Antonia say. Sounds of shushing, chairs being scraped, glasses collected. 'Goodnight all', a voice called out. Somebody turned off the light. The terrace was quiet.

A wind had sprung up.

High above her the giant she-oak rustled. It scraped an arm across the roof of the shed. A ripple seemed to run around the garden. Daytime trees and bushes withdrew into dodging outlines, dark, fitful, private. Even the daisies in the rockery swayed dead-white, to themselves. And the sprinkler rearing in the middle of the lawn, the silver pyramid of the Hills Hoist, the two bins sentried at the back steps, gleamed with their own taut power.

You had to cross the lawn with a steady forward tread, eyes straight ahead, just to get yourself inside.

New Year

1.

They are in the middle of a heatwave. All across the city people are doing unusual things. Walking into fountains, sleeping on the beach, holding conversations under a sprinkler . . . 'It's the heat': don't the Arabs have a wind, Rowena is trying to think of the name of it, a desert wind, so hot that a man is excused for killing his wife while it is blowing?

Harry and Rowena are having dinner with the Hutchisons. This is not unusual, since they live in the Hutchisons' house and share most meals with them: but it's New Year's Eve and here they are on the terrace, legs looped over chairs, opening their second bottle of wine. Festive yet resigned, like workers choosing to drink together after a hard day. The Hutchisons have chosen to stay home with Harry and Rowena tonight. This is what is unusual.

This is what Rowena thinks, stirring Harry's chicken stock in the kitchen. The kitchen is a glassed-in verandah three steps up from the terrace. Tonight it is a little box lit up with heat. Grease glistens in beads behind the stove. Oily fingers seem to have smeared everything, handles, cookery books, jars of herbs. Vine leaves over the terrace drape around the windows, limp and still, dropped hands.

The chicken stock is for pilau, Harry's speciality. Later Rowena, who doesn't have a speciality, will make a fruit salad. It's their turn to cook tonight.

Although Rowena likes watching stock, it's slow rich bubble, she knows it does not really need stirring. She is really listening out for her baby Tom. If she can get to him quickly when he wakes — he wakes a great deal — she might be able to settle him back to sleep. Meanwhile she gives a few busy taps to the saucepan with the side of the spoon.

'The person who really needs a drink', Hutch calls out, 'is Rowena'.

Lately Rowena has suspected a consensus in the house about her, about maternal over-commitment. Her case has been discussed, heads shaken . . . coming down the kitchen steps now as this person is not quite real to her. She feels a fruitless swinging to her arms, she is breasting dark air. She sits down quickly.

'This is very civilised', Harry is saying. He has just taken off his T-shirt and he stretches out, rubbing the fan of black hair that spouts up over his waistband.

'Hardly civilised', Hutch says, 'taking off your clothes'. He has a way of drawing out the Australian accent that makes everything he says sound measured and judicious.

'Let's face it', Harry says, 'we're a hedonist culture. On a night like this we ought to take off the lot.' His hand hovers for a moment over the front stud of his jeans.

'D'you hear what your husband's proposing?' Hutch turns to Rowena. She has no answer. She never has an answer for Hutch.

'Diane has more of the hedonist spirit', says Harry. Diane is wearing a sarong hitched up and looped around her neck like a miniature toga.

'Oh for heaven's sake', says Diane, rearranging her legs. 'It's *hot.*'

'Or is she just going with the au-naturel flow of our household?' Hutch says to Harry.

'I'll drink to that', says Harry. Across the table his torso is white amongst the shadows of the terrace. Winter white. Like her own hands around her glass. It had stopped being winter when they first arrived here from the beach house. They had stood beside their car in the mild city air, pale, in coats, as if they had come a long way . . .

'What are you looking at?' Harry's voice is low across the table.

'My hands.'

'What's *wrong* with your hands?' Harry mutters. But a steady droning is rising from the house. Their eyes lift and meet. Tom.

'Already?' Diane says. 'He's incredible.'

'He fell asleep early', Rowena says on her way back up the steps. 'It's the heat . . .' But who would understand the logic and rhythm of Tom's day? Who would want to? She takes her glass with her.

'How about some music', Hutch is saying.

'It's your *turn',* Diane says.

2.

In that house music was kept going like a tribal fire. Whoever came home first went straight to the living-room and put on music. The speakers were lugged up and down the hall on long cords, following the action. When they left again Rowena let the music die. There were many arrivals and departures. The Hutchisons were both studying part-time. They belonged to societies, separately, they went to films and rock concerts. Harry often went with them.

In the weekends they were careful to keep the sound well stoked. Music nudged away each moment, bit at the fringes of thought. Open the bedroom door and you swam wordless into it. The first nights they were here Rowena went walking. Up the empty street. Turn the corner. Drawn curtains at the end of driveways silhouetted with shrubs. Silence. Block after block of it. The beat of the music met her again on the home stretch. Their house looked party bright. She sat on the front steps and leaned her head against a column. It seemed to have caught a pulse inside it. She watched the light behind the roofs of the houses across the road. She didn't know where else to go.

Now as Tom sucks, his head seems to pump back and forward against her, in time. Their room is another piece of the verandah, a partitioned cavern. Curtainless, it is dark all day, shadowed by the house next door, but at night the neighbours' bathroom light beacons through the louvres and everything, the cartons from the beach house stacked around the walls, Harry's shirt dangling from the door frame, the roundness of Tom's head, is outlined in this dull radiance.

Last night, lying like this on the mattress, she had said to Harry: 'How much longer are we going to stay here?'

Harry had just shut his book, put out the light and turned over: there was a sense of purpose about everything he did these days, even to going to sleep. He turned onto his back and unfolded one finger, two, as if they had been waiting to spring open.

'We're still paying off the bookshop.' He had to whisper. Behind the wall next to them were the Hutchisons, also in bed. 'We could never afford to live like this so close to the city.' End of point two: he closed his hand into a fist over their sheet.

'I could live in a tiny flat', Rowena said. Whispering was provisional, it was like taking off your shoes and tiptoeing around each other. 'I could live in a room. If we were alone.'

'We're always alone', Harry said.

Tom sucks and, elbow up, she sips her wine.

3.

The light is on under the vines of the terrace but nobody is there. Moths bang against the light bulb and fall among the glasses on the table. Somebody has watered the ferns and they rustle and drip around the steps. Intermission. This happens sometimes. Everybody will suddenly desert on private missions, to read the newspaper, make a phone call, slump across a bed . . . The light is on in the kitchen too. Harry is cooking.

He looks up as Rowena comes up the steps, his chin lifted, eyes gathered together to hold in the tears. But it will do for a greeting, it is so familiar. Onions. He turns back to his chopping board. Steam rises, oil sizzles ready, his strokes are neat and sure. Harry cooks with a sense of ceremony. Step by step, a beautiful patient logic towards a known destination: no panicky improvisations, no peering at the recipe wishing it would tell you more.

He is singing, a beat behind and lower than the larger voice that fills the room beyond them.

'Still crazy,
Still crazy,
After all these years . . .'

Harry singing, onions frying: Rowena stands for a moment in the doorway. He has always sung, to car radios, in supermarkets and restaurants, easily, knowing the words, 'Yesterday', 'O Sole Mio', 'You Are So Beautiful', as if in tune with a fellow experience.

'Want some help?'

He never says he does.

The Hutchisons' house is old, one day they are going to knock it down. Meanwhile they have hung mounted posters of things like sneakers and Coca-Cola bottles on the stucco walls. Leads and aerials loop between picture railings. The mantel pieces are cluttered with jokey plunder: KEEP LEFT and NO SMOKING signs, a Chinese demon kite, a Snoopy mug half full of small change. But the rooms remain dark and sedate; tonight each is a cell of hot still air. The two visions of the house don't match, they are overlaid like illusionist sheets, demand something of you . . . a trick of wit, Rowena feels, and she would see it as a style.

The front door is open, the steps of the porch are still warm. Rowena lights a cigarette. She has taken up smoking again.

'Are these for real?' she had asked Hutch, pointing at the NO SMOKING signs.

'Why else would they be there?' Hutch said.

Why else did Rowena, finding an old packet of cigarettes in Harry's winter jacket, take one out and smoke it? The air before her lifted and shook. She took another one. This time it tasted more real, the house seemed to retreat behind the fraying coil of smoke. She bought her own packet. She enjoyed the crackle as she opened it, the neat decision of the cylinders stacked as close as bullets. She took to carrying a packet in the pouch pocket of her overalls. At odd moments, outside the house, she smoked them.

Just as she lights up now, Hutch breaks through the darkness at the side of the house, pulling a hose. In the other hand he carries his glass of wine. He doesn't seem to see her, but if she wasn't there would he stroll across the lawn like this, taking sips as he plants the sprinkler near her and turns on the tap? He suddenly sinks beside her.

'Very contemplative', he says. 'You're always very contemplative Rowena.'

The sprinkler's arms have corralled them against the porch. Water patters at their feet. Hutch is always setting up these little moments with her and she always comes away feeling she has failed a test.

'The madonna', Hutch says. 'I take it that's what you want to be.'

His voice has dropped, his blonde head is bowed towards her. Rowena hunches her shoulders. She will not look at him.

'Dinner', she says, waving her arm vaguely, getting up. 'Must help Harry.' Her voice is husky, out of practice. She throws her cigarette into the garden and then remembers it is his garden and makes a little useless dive mid-air. She closes her eyes for a moment on her way back up the hall. She should have stamped the butt out at his feet, raised her eyebrows, stalked off . . . Why? Because he would have liked that? In this house value is given to performance.

Just as Harry places the big platter of yellow rice on the terrace table, Tom wakes. A loud outraged howl this time.

'Oh God', Diane says. 'How do you bear it?'

Harry serves, and Rowena hands out plates.

'Maybe I'm just not the type', Diane goes on. She picks up her fork with her narrow freckled hand, looks around the table. She often has this moment of animation when a plate of food is put in front of her, Rowena has noticed. 'Why do people *do* this to themselves d'you think?'

'Because they don't know what they're letting themselves in for', Harry says.

Hutch stands up, turning and turning at the corkscrew embedded in the bottle between his legs. They all watch, wait for the triumphant Pop! 'Tight one', Hutch says, chasing sweat across his forehead in a kind of salute.

Tom's cry is urgent. Rowena drains her glass, reaches over and takes a forkful of pilau from the platter. She won't be back for a while.

'All I know is', Diane says, turning to her plate, 'nobody could ever make me miss my meal'.

'Go on', Harry says to Rowena. 'We'll leave you some.'

4.

One night Harry came home very late to the beach house. It was so black outside you could imagine that he might never find them again, the frail house could disappear into a shifting fold of the dunes . . . He would have phoned, if of course there was a phone . . . it was becoming bloody impossible . . . he swayed slightly above her and Tom in the bed. He'd been drinking with Hutch and his wife, he'd been thinking . . . The Hutchisons said, come and live with them, they're interested in sharing . . . No the Hutchisons have no children. But a child shouldn't make any difference, they said.

Harry seemed to have forgotten that he used to say that too.

There are photos — here, kept close beside the bed — of the time that they first brought Tom home to the beach house. In this bright darkness the black and white leap out at you as if in moonlight. They are good photos of Rowena because she has at last stopped looking at the camera. She is smiling, she can't stop smiling, looking at Tom in her arms. Her hair, which reaches to her elbows, is now tucked back out of the way. She's wearing overalls, but you can see that her breasts are enormous. In the background a ti-tree brushes against asbestos. That's the beach house.

The photos of Harry with Tom are slightly out of focus. Rowena took them. There was no one else around to take them all together, *en famille.* The blurring gives the impression of a high wind. Harry is bending over Tom in his pram as if he's sheltering him. He is frowning in a comic-father way. The ti-tree appears to be in violent action, caught up in a storm. But you can see that the cigarette Harry holds behind him is still alight.

The bathroom of the beach house was separate, a quick dash from the back door. When one of them wanted a shower the other had to be there to feed the chip heater. The heater roared, the pipes shuddered, draughts rushed in through the warped door. Spiders rocked their cradles of dead blowflies in amongst the steam.

Bent over the heater one morning she thought she heard Harry groan.

'What's the matter?'

He stood still. He was wearing her shower cap. Water ran on and on, clung to the tip of his nose, the panels of black hair on his shoulders, his chest, above his penis, swirled about his feet. He looked straight ahead, through water.

He didn't go to the shop that morning. He went to bed. He stayed there for nine days. It wouldn't matter, nobody came anyway, he said. (Second-hand books! Out there! You must be crazy, everyone had said when he set up the shop.) He slept for twelve hours at a time.

Tom cried and cried. She walked him up and down the verandah, around the peripheries of the house. It might be after midday before she could get dressed. When he slept she lay on the couch with him in the crook of her arm, like a book.

Sand crept in under the doors. Mice scrabbled, but she could not bear to set the traps. Every living creature reminded her of Tom. The fridge went empty. From time to time she found herself before the open kitchen cupboard eating nuts and raisins fist after fist. She trod carefully past

Harry's door. It seemed to take her whole being just to keep Tom alive.

When Harry was awake she sat on the end of the gritty bed, feeding Tom.

'Do something different!' Harry said, sitting up, smoking, watching her with glittering eyes. 'Is this all you ever do? Surprise me! Surprise me sometimes why don't you.'

(He didn't remember saying any of this, later on.)

A storm passed quickly on the beach front. You saw it coming, a mist wiping out the horizon ruled across the windows, whiteness on whiteness, while somewhere a blind flapped, louvres rattled, trees grew furtive. The voice outside took over, the house was hollowed into darkness, din, like a loss of consciousness: five minutes and it was over, a bird sang, the radio spoke again.

Harry got a job with the Government. In the mornings the car steamed as he encouraged Tom to wave bye-bye. It would be well after dark by the time he got back from the city. He made friends with someone called Hutchison, his age, but a senior administrator in the department. He stopped taking a packed lunch. He gave up smoking.

In the late afternoon the wind dropped and Rowena and Tom went walking. Down the carefully curved roads, some still gravel, named 'Pleasant Drive' or 'Linden Way'. It was all allotments, waiting to become numbered houses in a suburb; flowers grew among scrub and hillocks, tough, close-clustered, with a medicinal perfume that scented the dunes. When she picked them she could feel the shadow of clouds moving across the sunlight on her bent back.

At this hour retired couples came out like moths and walked arm in arm towards the glow settling over the sea. The rattle of the pram echoed behind them. They turned to smile at her from their end of the road.

The beach itself was unspectacular, edged with seaweed and miniature limestone cliffs. The winter sea was milk-turquoise, a great bowl in sluggish motion.

The sun glares low over the horizon, shows its power, the sea is a silver reflection, the road gleams, dances with struck flint, Rowena has to half shut her eyes. The wind presses against her, against her eyes and mouth so that she is smiling, blinded over the pram, and yes, she is happy, in some way about as happy as she can be.

The wine has spread through her.

Tom's head is slumped back like a drunk's, around it the dim bedroom, the house, the music, the lit heads on the terrace spin out in a circle.

5.

It is as hot outside as in.

'*Good* evening!' Hutch calls out as Rowena stands blinking on the steps. 'I was just volunteering to go and wake you up.' He pulls out a chair for her with his foot.

'There's plenty left', Harry says, waving his hand over the table. It doesn't look appetising. Amongst the spilled glasses, the plates scattered with grains of rice and chicken bones, moths are dragging in circles, grounded in pools of amber oil.

'Aren't you hot in those overalls?' Diane asks. Her legs are spread, she is fanning herself with a sandal.

'Take 'em off', shouts Harry.

Their faces under the light look yellowish and greasy. Their eyes have almost disappeared.

'Wine', Harry says, searching for a glass for her. 'Wonderful wine.' His mouth is faintly rimmed with black.

'Eases the pressure of family life', says Hutch.

Rowena starts collecting plates.

'Just relax', Hutch says.

'Moths', Rowena says. She sees Tom's head lolling, a dark spot on their bed where she has left him.

Rowena is making fruit salad. Watermelon, rock melon, grapes, peaches, passionfruit, mangoes, plums: she has taken them out of their stained brown paper bags and lined them up on the bench. Whether to make it minimal and chic, just the melon and grapes say, or to throw in everything . . . Rowena has an idea, she has seen a picture somewhere, the watermelon carved like a bowl, the fruits spilling out of it . . .

The big knife has made her bold, slicing through cheeks of pink flesh . . . it comes away from the rinds with a sucking sound . . . take it all off . . . and then chop, chop into children's blocks, pink, all shades of pink, orange, tawny . . . The music throbs, Rowena chops, she is hot, she has never felt so hot. The kitchen is so crowded, its bin is overflowing, the benches are covered with plates, scraps, fruit . . . she has to work on a chopping board balanced on a chair, crouching, so that the buckles of her overalls bite into her, she can hardly move or breathe . . .

It is so simple. It works with the speed of a good idea. To unbuckle. Unpeel. To step out of the overalls, kick at them, and feel that trusty roughness, thigh against thigh. She gathers up rinds, pips, peel, and dumps them in the sink. Why stop there? Already she is moving easily, the T-shirt slips easily up her spine, cooling it, releasing her head. It's as if a breeze is suddenly blowing all over her body. She's in a hurry now. A glass splinters outside and there's laughter. *Wait.* Her breasts come loping out of their milk-stiffened cups, she could almost fear for them as she bends over her knife . . . the final touches . . . pants, you need two hands and they're over your knees, binding them, but — you just step out of them . . . She's wading in her own clothes, hands plunged up to the wrists in fruit, mixing it, the passionfruit sprays out as she squeezes its upturned pouch . . . She washes her hands.

Here is Rowena, descending a staircase, her bowl held out before her, while somewhere over towards the city there is a rude outbreak of car horns. New Year. She is only aware of the whiteness beneath her, this company of globes and triangles, trusting them with her own grave progress.

And the faces looking up at her are frozen, their mouths are frozen open as if they cannot open wide enough for the laughter, they are stamping their feet, clutching their chairs with laughter, like uncles who have had one of their own tricks played on them. Tears run down Harry's face. Hutch claps.

Something white flies by and catches on the vines. Clothing? Actions bring results . . . but she is beginning to feel a drop, a fatal fading of interest. She has already been delivered of one miracle. She is tired. She places the watermelon bowl on the table in front of Harry.

'Here you are', she says.

The Girls Love Each Other

The girls love each other these days. That's what I told Beth last week. She'd just got back from Bali and we were having one of our catch-up sessions: Beth comes into the salon at eight and we talk our heads off while I give her a shampoo and brush-up before work. By half past there's cold coffee and cigarette ash and photos all over the bench. We're always frantic — that's our word — but it's our only time to really talk since Beth moved in with Douglas, and I've got Morveen at home most of the time. With friends.

That's what I was trying to talk about with Beth. That was my news. After she'd shown me her tan (she was worried she was *too* dark), and given me my carving and the batik for Morveen and gone on about all the tourists who'd been after Mardi's body and even hers — I told her that I was sharing my house with *three* unemployed teenage girls.

'Jan, you're too easy-going', Beth said, for about the thousandth time. Two weeks alone with Mardi (her daughter, Morveen's age) had been enough for her, thank you, though they'd had their good times too, some good talks. I started to say that yes, so had we, it was interesting in a way.

'Actually', Beth went on, bending her head away from the blower, 'it's not the girls so much I mind, it's all the boyfriends hanging round'.

'There's no boyfriends', I said. I was standing over Beth, layering up her left side, she's got lovely hair, coarse, blonde, shapes up beautifully. Then I found myself saying it, as if it had been on my mind all the time: 'The girls love each other these days'.

There was just that moment when Beth looked up and caught my eye waiting in the mirror, and looked down again. Ticking back over ten years like I'd been doing.

'First I've heard of it', she said.

Morveen and Mardi practically share a birthday — they're both Leos — but it took Beth and me quite a time to give up on pretending they were friends. They learned ballet and tap together until Morveen just wouldn't get into the car one day. And in the school holidays Beth and I would take a day off and drag the girls round town to lunch and a matinee. 'Go on your own', they told us in the end. Then by the time Mardi was fourteen you'd have thought she was twenty: she's working out at Channel 9 now and the trip to Bali was the prize for the Beach Queen heat last year.

Morveen's like me, no show pony, she doesn't even try. But up to now there's always been this little thing between Beth and me, that our girls were in the same race, only Morveen was shy and young for her age.

I suddenly remembered how different Beth and I were. How when we used to work together at Max's she wouldn't talk to any of the clients she thought were 'weirdos', and called old Max 'the poofter' behind his back. And how she just doesn't say anything about Morveen going on the dole when she could have got a place in the Teachers' College. Morveen had said she wanted a break to think things over, and I know what she means. I'd wanted that too once, and then when Johnny my son left, I'd *had* to have it — Morveen's had a lot to handle, one way or another. There are some things Beth doesn't understand.

'You know', I started, though I didn't know what I was going to say. But Beth jumped up, she had to rush, she was frantic, she had to be in Perth by nine (she's a cosmetic rep these days) and Douglas had asked all these people over for drinks that night.

'Sure you won't come?' she asked, patting her hair in the mirror. 'Bring Bradley? How is he these days?'

'I haven't seen him for a while', I said, 'since the girls came'.

'Take care', she said (it's one of Douglas's expressions). We kissed each other at the door.

Friday is our busy day at the salon, but every time I turned on the blower I was taken back to what I'd said to Beth. I thought about the girls. How they just seemed to appear in my life, sitting round the kitchen table. I'd been to a movie with Bradley: we nearly fell over a couple of duffle bags in the hall. Then we saw these three cropped heads turning towards us at the kitchen door. Morveen had a little glittery catch in her eyes that she gets when she's pleased about something.

It turned out that Steph is a sort of cousin by friendship. Lily Carson, her grandmother, was my mother's best friend. I just remember Lily before she moved to Sydney, but something about Steph's neat sharp face and her quick way of talking reminded me of her.

'Yeah, everyone says that', Steph said. It seemed that Linda, Steph's friend, who's got a soft baby face and smokes a lot, had been having hassles with the Youth Hostel. They'd been telling Morveen about it. They wondered if. . . . So I said they could have Johnny's room.

Bradley didn't stay long. It didn't feel right somehow, to go into the lounge with the whisky and close the sliding doors like we usually do. He stood up and straightened his jacket and said: 'Goodnight . . . girls'.

'Night', they said, hardly looking at him.

At the door he said: 'Be careful Janet. Don't let them take advantage of you.' We didn't make any plans for the next weekend.

It soon became clear that the last thing those girls wanted was to take advantage of a fellow woman. They decided that since I was the worker they would do all the shopping and cooking and washing-up.

'That's how a co-operative works', Linda explained to me.

'In some circumstances', I said, 'it's also called marriage'.

'We're not asking you for sexual favours', Steph said

with a little smile.

But it worked out pretty well. In fact shopping and cooking seemed to be all they did do.

'It's such lovely weather', I said, 'and you've hardly seen anything of Perth'.

'Depends what you're interested in', Steph said. She smiled at Morveen and me. She's got a lovely smile.

Some nights they borrowed my old Torana and went to hear some music in a pub or see a film in Fremantle. Mostly they sat around talking. On nights that we were all at home I seemed to be expected to join in. I must say there was something about the way Steph gave you all her attention, with big nods at everything you'd say, that really got you going. I'd never heard Morveen talk as much either.

Steph tackled me about my job. How did I feel, she asked, that as a hairdresser, I basically 'exploited the beauty trip' that men laid on women? I said that most of my clients at 'Janette's' were older women coming in for a trim or a perm. 'Nobody wants hair down to their ankles', I said.

'Come on Jan, I'm talking about fashion.'

'Look at you three, that's a fashion isn't it? Who cuts your hair anyway?'

'It's not fashion, it's anti-fashion. It's cut by a friend in Sydney who's dropped out of the straight hair-dressing scene.'

'And it *feels* good', put in Linda.

'So does my hair', I said. 'And I can blow-dry it in a few minutes.'

'Whether you know it or not', Steph said, 'you wear it like that to attract men'.

'Yeah', said Morveen.

'Well who are you trying to attract with your hairdos then?' I said 'Each other?'

They seemed to think this was a huge joke. Linda started to clap and knocked her drink over Steph's record.

'By the way', Steph said, grabbing the record off Linda and wiping it without looking at her, 'I need a trim. You wouldn't . . .?'

'No I wouldn't', I said.

It was good for Morveen and me, having the others there. It was a relief not to come home and find her sleeping with five apple-cores beside her bed. Or hear the fridge door open and close all evening while she ate as if she had to save her life.

When had I last heard her hum like she did when she was cooking the co-operative meals? I guess it was when she was a kid and she'd come in after Johnny had taken her for a ride on his bike. She's never been one for smiling much — all chins and frown as a baby — but when we'd all been talking and it was getting late, she had this sort of sleepy soft look about her, and she'd rest her head on the nearest shoulder. When it was mine I wanted to stop talking, everything, and put my arms around her, but I'm not that silly.

I found out that all this time she'd never liked her name.

'It was your grandmother's name', I said. 'It's Welsh.'

'So?' she said. 'I don't like it. *Mor — veen.'* She beat her fist on the table in time and and glared at me. 'Mor — veen — Jones.' Bang, bang, bang.

'I never thought of it like that', I said. Lennie had wanted it, and then it had become part of a different sound, 'Johnny and Morveen', the sound that kept me going.

But the next time I came home I heard Steph say quite casually as she put on a record, 'Do you know this one Veen?' From then on it was 'Veen this' and 'Veen that'. No one said a word about it.

The story of my marriage went down very well. They sat there shaking their heads through the saga of Lennie and his disappearing act. Linda jumped up and started massaging my neck. Not that their own family histories sounded much better. Though I must say it surprised me that a son of old Lily Carson would be a 'mental wife-beater' and an 'alcoholic capitalist exploiter'. His wife's only sin seemed to be that she 'freshened up before hubby came home'. I don't suppose I came off any better when I'd gone to work.

Then the last Saturday before they went, I was lying out the back in my bikini, soaking up the lovely late summer sun. Even my face, though Beth's told me off about that often enough. I still get a kick out of my backyard after all those years in the flat. It's just a big square of brown grass sloping down to an old peppermint tree by the fence.

Then I heard the crying. It was coming from Johnny's room on the back verandah. Not just crying, but an awful rising wail that seemed to curl around my stomach. I picked it out, like you do with little children, as Linda's voice. I sat up and everything went blurry. I heard the other two run in to her. She screamed 'You!' There was talking, and the crying dropped away.

It was all over in a minute. I lay down again but my stomach kept on tightening. I could see our washing dancing at me on the line, the girls' big clown clothes flapping against my uniforms and panty-hose and bras. After a while I made my way inside. I just kept thinking, I don't know, I don't know anything.

I took the girls out to the bus station on Saturday afternoon, as soon as I got home from work. The co-operative had been winding down that last week, the girls had gone out a lot more. I was glad, I was tired: even at work I seemed to be hearing their young voices all day, back and forth with mine.

They didn't talk much in the car. Every time I'd say something to Morveen next to me, she'd say 'What?' She kept looking out the window, humming.

At the bus station Steph fished out their tickets from the little purse she wears looped around her waist, and Linda queued with their bags. There seemed to be a rhythm going round between them all. I watched Steph, standing there with her head just nodding and one foot tapping away in its old tennis shoe. I thought, she's so sure. She's dangerous.

They stood waiting for the call then, the three of them, with their arms around one another. When it was time to go there were big serious hugs all round.

'Jan, thank you', Linda said through tears. I watched them darting off behind the other passengers, like children. When I turned, I found that Morveen had already set off. I saw her striding ahead of me towards the car.

It seemed so quiet at home that afternoon, you could hear the peppermint tree tossing about in the wind. Morveen went straight to her room. I couldn't settle to anything. I put a few things back to their old places in the kitchen. In the end I jumped in the shower. Then Morveen stuck her head round the door and said: 'It's the big B for you on the phone'.

Bradley's voice seemed to come from another world. I stood there watching the mist spread out from my hot toes over the polished boards. He was trying to let me know how busy he'd been these past weeks.

'Are you all right?' he asked.

'I've missed you.'

There was a pause. Then very gruff he said:

'Pick you up at eight then — sweetie'.

Morveen came into the hall.

'Are you going out tonight?' The same old question.

'Yes', I said. 'Are you?'

'I'm not into socialising, just for the sake of it.'

'Some of us actually enjoy a man's company from time to time. Drinking and talking like you've been doing every night.'

'We had real talk. But Bradley's a shithead. They've all been shitheads, you know that.'

'Don't you think', I said at last, 'that there's any good men around?'

'Well one thing's for sure', she said, walking off. 'I don't need them.'

I headed outside then and sat on the front steps, still in my dressing gown. There are no houses in front of us, just a lovely stretch of sky over the railway line. The street lights had come on and the evening traffic was starting up. I watched the cars, joined up by headlights, filing towards the subway.

Saturday nights. The city. Morveen always hated me going out in the old days. She'd scream and scream so Johnny'd have to take her for a ride around the block while Beth and I drove off. 'She's just jealous', Beth would say, accelerating. 'You deserve a bit of fun.'

Morveen hated me talking on the phone too, those long

sessions picking up the pieces after all the fun. Every two minutes one of us would have to break off to hiss and slap and bribe with biscuits, just to stay on that life-line, just to say: 'Do you know what that bastard said to me?'

And now here was Morveen saying she could do without all that. You could hardly blame her. I think her view's lopsided: she thinks mine is. We're opposite each other like a pair of scales. But for a long time my side carried the weights. Maybe Morveen was pushed out of balance, right from the start.

I *had* learnt some things. Not enough for Morveen now, not enough to even up. But I learned to pay my own way. In the beginning, when I married Lennie Jones, I thought that from then on I'd be taken care of. Even afterwards, when I was alone, I had my sheikh dream. I'd be walking to the bus-stop after work (Jan, you get along now, Max'd always say, dead on five, I'd spend all year wondering what I could buy him for Christmas), two buses I needed to get the kids home, and I'd think that if a big fat sheikh pulled up beside me in a limousine, I'd just crawl right in. 'Come on kids', I'd say. 'We're going to live in a harem. Won't that be fun?'

Beth came along and she taught me: you always pay your own way. Now I didn't ask for much, just my own place, and a chat with Beth, and Bradley turning up from time to time.

Bradley's a shithead. Well I know what she means. You think he's good-looking, so clean and well-cut, till you get up close and there's something missing in his face, he has to practise looking you in the eye. And practise having what he calls his 'R and R': he fits me in between badminton and bushwalks, and then cuts everything short to get a good night's sleep. He can't cope otherwise, he says. Well, that's how he is.

So why do I bother? Just sometimes, out of the blue, driving home late, or having breakfast, once when we were standing in a queue, I start to tease him, I can't stop myself, I'm laughing like nothing matters any more. And he bends his head to me (he's very tall) and calls me a terrible girl, and keeps looking at me sideways in a shy, pleased way . . . So I hang in there, while the weeks build up again between us, work and the telephone, dinner and a show. Waiting for those real times again.

Morveen was sitting beside me in the dark.

'Jan. I'm going to Sydney.'

'When?' The stars seemed tiny above the lights on the road.

'As soon as I can get my act together.'

'What'll you do there?'

'Live with the others. They've got a big place, there's six of them.'

'Six girls', I said.

'I'll look for work of course. I'm not going to bludge forever.'

'Six girls, in a house. Don't you think that's a bit . . . narrow?'

'People come and go a lot, Steph says. Anyway, what are you trying to say?'

'I dunno love. It's not my way I guess.' *You pay for your choices,* I wanted to say.

Morveen had put her arm around me.

'Mum, why don't you come over when I'm settled and have a holiday? We'd have a good time I know. We could look for Johnny . . . Steph and Linda reckon you should.'

'Thanks love. I'll think about it.'

Morveen jumped up soon and went inside. She couldn't keep still for long that night.

I felt very tired out there. Too tired to get ready for Bradley. It was getting cold.

The phone rang. Beth.

'I know this is an awful time to ring', she said as usual. 'It's just that I'm feeling so *flat.'*

'That makes two of us.'

Then she was off. Douglas hadn't come home yet, he was on his high horse, he said she drank too much when she was with his friends. Who were so boring anyway . . .

'Honestly Jan, sometimes I miss the old days. When you and I used to hit the town. I think I'm a romantic at heart.'

Also her tan was peeling, and Mardi was off looking for a flat. 'God knows what she'll get up to then', she said.

In the kitchen Morveen had switched on the light and the

radio. I smelt scrambled eggs and I felt like a glass of wine. This was something that seemed to stretch right back to Mum and Lily Carson. A kind of talk. I'd been speaking it for years now at the back of all the heads of those faces in the mirror.

'Hold on a sec Beth', I said. I whipped into the kitchen and filled up a glass from the cask with a wink at Morveen.

'Anyway, how's things with you?' Beth asked. You always have to remind her that you've got a life ticking away there too. 'How's Morveen and the girls?'

'The girls have gone back to Sydney', I said, 'and Morveen's going to go over there too'. I took a deep sip while Beth went on about how they all leave us and how we'd probably end up in a Home together.

'Morveen wants me to come over for a holiday.'

'Yeah?' said Beth, listening.

'I dunno, I'd have to get someone in at the salon, and it might put Bradley out a bit, and I'm tired, there doesn't seem much point . . .'

'Well hang it all', Beth said, out of the silence. 'Hang it all, why don't you go?'

Enough Rope

Every now and then an energy builds up in me and I know that it's time to visit Michael. Quite suddenly everything, the set of rooms I move through, the seesaw glare and darkness as I pass outside and in, the glint of the dam down on the boundary, becomes the background to a dream.

I rush the boys off to the school-bus and throw my packed bag into the car. Ian just watches me. But we've finished seeding and I haven't visited my mother for a long time.

At the first roadhouse in the metropolitan area I ring Michael at the school where he is teaching.

'Oh hello', he says. I can hear the faint, endless barracking of children in a playground. 'Tonight? Yes, fine, see you then.' He could be making an appointment with an anxious parent.

I always arrive rather windswept on Michael's doorstep. This is a tradition. It is not windy on the quiet streets of Lakeside Estate where Michael has lived since his marriage. But he used to live on the top floor of a block of flats with a cosmopolitan's-eye view of Perth. In those days, when the boys were very young, I was always late. I would stand for a moment in the cold tunnels of city air and study the careful schoolteacher script of *M. Makevis* beside the door.

I still wear an air of haste and escape now, dodging among the hanging baskets on Michael's discreet front porch. It is a form of apology. I juggle with my bottles in their damp paper sleeves — beer, wine or champagne, I try to vary them so as not to look too predictable.

'Bon soir', says Michael, while his door-chimes are still pealing. This greeting is again a tradition. Years ago at teachers' college, we liked to season our exchanges with 'adieu' and 'merci bien' and 'c'est pas mal tu sais'. Unlike the French however, we do not kiss on meeting. It leaves, has always left, a tiny gap, during which Michael takes my bottles into the kitchen and I try to decide where to sit.

There is something deliberate about Michael's clatter in the kitchen.

'Is Lauren home?' I call across the bar.

'She's rehearsing.' He brings in our drinks. 'She's got a recital next week.'

She wasn't home the last time I visited either.

'Your house is looking great', I say, though in this dimmed light I can't notice any change. Couches seem to grow out of the pale carpet. The smoky glass of the coffee table is still unsmudged and bare. It stretches between us, shin to shin. His are crossed, in pale jeans.

'We finished the music room last week.' He puts down his drink. 'Would you like to have a look?'

For the first time he leads me into the private part of his house. An old sensation of conspiracy unfolds as I follow him down a corridor. We used to stifle laughter in my mother's kitchen once, making coffee late at night. Something about the cannisters' diminuendo from big FLOUR to little TEA . . .

'. . . but the view'll improve when the trees have grown', he is saying. We are crossing a little courtyard. I glimpse a plastic washing basket, an upturned mop, ordinary domesticity. 'She always hated me listening when she practised.' He smiles at this over his shoulder as he unlocks the door.

The music room smells new, of pine and cement. Lauren's baby grand stands sleek and black in the middle of the room. There is an old couch under a bare window. Michael stays by the door.

'I bet Lauren's in here all the time', I say, opening the

piano.

'Not a great deal yet.' His hand is on the light switch, ready to go. 'She's very involved with this Bach group. Out nearly every night. Though she's got a friend, a flautist, who comes over in the day sometimes to play duets.'

He locks the door again as we go out.

'How are the boys?'

This is better. We are on sure ground here. For Michael this is no routine enquiry. They are restless, I say, and too rough with each other at the moment. Ian says they need pulling into line. My voice is hesitant. I think they're bored at school.

Michael nods. He starts talking about his class. The theme this term is the planets: the space-ship they're building is becoming more complex than he can always understand. It incorporates the school computer. The boys in his class are working really well together since they started this project.

I say I do not think Miss MacPherson at the Yardoo Primary goes in for the space age. 'I wish *you* taught the boys.' I think I say this every time I see him. And he just gives the same half smile and goes on talking. Of course. Even as a student Michael had his own ideas. I listened, but ended up going with the stream: *don't let the little bastards get you down.*

I think about the time I brought the boys here to see Michael. As usual we were staying with my mother.

'You certainly have your hands full', my mother always says.

Michael had taped the World Cup soccer final ready for them on his video. He showed them how to make a milkshake.

'Wow this place is like that T.V. commercial', I heard them tell him in the kitchen. They swivelled on his bar-stools and tried their jokes on him.

'Can we go to Michael's?' they still ask me when we're driving to the city.

Michael is still talking. This year he has been posted to a school in a wealthy middle-class area. The kids are great —

Michael always says this about his classes, they're *his* kids now — but there are different sorts of problems. Some of the parents push their children, ask Michael when he'll be giving the class real work to do.

'Have I told you this already?'

'No no, go on.' I can watch him as I used to when he talked. In winter his face is so pale it's almost luminous. 'Milkface': that's what the kids called him when he first came to Australia. He stood on the edge of the playground in the shorts made by his mother and saw that no one else wore shorts below the knee. He told me that once.

'Things are changing', he is saying. 'I think the children are the only ones who can keep up.' Now he's cupped his palm and balanced his empty glass on it. 'But you have to trust them, you have to let them go a bit . . .' He flicks his glass with his other hand and strikes a precarious note.

Michael and Lauren have no children. This has never surprised me although they've been married for some years. Perhaps it's because I always think of Lauren as being very young. She must be in her late twenties now, but the last time I saw her she was as thin and childlike as ever. She has a little flat white face, with eyes and nose and mouth crowded together, and a bush of crinkly brown hair springing back from her forehead.

I couldn't say that I really know Lauren. When Michael wrote to tell me he was married, I arrived at the new house with champagne and a wedding present. Michael met me juggling a glass of dissolving disprin. Lauren had a headache, she was going to bed. She sat in a dressing-gown on the arm of his chair while he opened the present.

'Thanks very much', she said as she got up to leave.

She was very gifted, Michael explained in a low voice. Her mother had pushed her, practice six hours a day, no friends, talent quests, frilly dresses. It was amazing she still wanted to play at all. She was very strong really, knew what she wanted. He was helping her work towards that.

Yes, I'd said then, looking around me. Lakeside Estate. Full-page, colour supplement, *Where your dreams become realities.* We drank a toast to his marriage, smiling but not finding much to say.

I've never told Michael about the time I saw him and Lauren at the lake. We were down for the Show, I'd taken the boys there to let off steam. They disappeared, I sat in the car to look at people. It was a wet and windy Sunday afternoon. Some sort of a club, or an office on picnic, was playing a rather bossy game of cricket with an outfield of girlfriends slouching among the eskies. I saw them suddenly, weaving their way through the players. Their familiarity, Michael's leather jacket, Lauren's hunched shoulders and blowing woolly hair, materialised for me as if I'd been expecting them.

I saw Lauren break away, veer towards the lake, stand looking down with her hands in the pockets of her parka. Michael followed, said something to her, set off towards the kiosk. He walked right near my car on his way back to her. I saw that he was holding two icecreams. His head was bent and he had a little smile on his face. You've got your hands full Michael, I caught myself thinking.

Tonight Michael and I are shifting fast from second gear into third. We haven't got this far past the rituals for a long time. Michael's given up on getting drinks for us from his bar. He's put a flagon of wine and the whisky bottle on the table between us. Through it I discover an aquarium view of my blind stockinged feet.

Better make this my last, I think into my wine. Or second last. But already I'm feeling that gathering of cheer that means it could be too late for limits. Recently I've been rather pushing the limits, all around the district. *You* certainly enjoyed yourself, people tell me later. The end of every social occasion has been a blank. When I come to, I'm alone in a quietly throbbing car. Ian is outside, opening our gate in the moonlight. He gets back in the car, I shut my eyes, the car lurches forward, then throbs to itself again. I open my eyes. Ian is closing the gate. Limits.

I don't want Michael to know this. I don't want him to have to escort me reeling to the car. Or worse. Throwing up into his native garden. There's a lot I don't want him to know about me. My triviality. My laziness. How much I weigh. Our relationship, as I've often told myself, is characterised by a beautiful restraint.

Although tonight Michael himself is not holding back, I notice. As he leans forward to pour himself another whisky, a strand of hair falls across his forehead. He leaves it there. He rips open a packet of peanuts and makes an avalanche of them into a bowl. Both of us ladle up peanuts and munch in an absent-minded way.

'You know Michael', I say, 'there isn't one sign of Lauren in this room'.

He looks at me.

'Ah yes.' My remark hangs between us. 'Ah yes. My waiting room.'

'Oh I don't mean . . .'

'My waiting room. Where I *wait.'* There's that little smile again that creases up his eyes.

'Lauren's rehearsing . . .'

'Ah yes.' I don't recognise the new cut of his tone. It goes with the smile. *'And* Lauren cannot drive. Therefore the flautist must give her a lift. The Polish flautist.'

This time I say nothing.

'And I wait.' He says this to me as if I might accuse him of something.

Michael and I can't sit and face each other any more. Michael has wandered off somewhere. But first he's put on some soft jazz, as if to keep me company.

I'm sorry, I say across this room where I don't belong. I've never known what Michael wanted of me. Even if that meant keeping away.

What now? I lean back, shut my eyes, waiting. But my centre of gravity seems to have moved to my left ear. I slide my cheek down into the rough surface of Michael's couch. With one eye I survey a tweed horizon. I see the colours of the native garden growing across this suburban block. Grey sand laps the feet of a raw brown fence. Dull green nursery saplings shake their name-tags beside gravel paths. He says their names to himself as he passes. One day they will wave a private shelter around his house, her music room.

How do I know about waiting?

Once Michael and I sat in a cafe, saying goodbye. We had both just graduated. Michael was leaving for Europe the next day. I didn't know where I was going.

It was January, but it had been a day of freak tropical rain. Cars swished by outside in a luxuriant greenish twilight. The jukebox was playing bouzouki music, the cafe-owner smiled at us. We'd often sat here, it was one of the few places in this city with any atmosphere, we said. But this time Michael kept checking his watch. He showed me his ticket and stowed it away again with careful fingers.

'I'd better get you home. I'd better get myself home. My last night and all that.' He smiled at me for our old shared bondage. I did not respond. Our widowed mothers sat on opposite sides of the city. His mother wore black, served sweet black coffee in tiny cups, spoke in another language. But about the same things, Michael said. Probed and warned, chased up lineages. We had been encircled. But he was getting away.

I couldn't look at him. This new, harder presence, no longer attending me, was suddenly proof of its own value. I felt him at the edge of my shoulder, at the tips of my fingers, at arm's length where I had been so careful to keep him. Quiet, pale Michael Makevis.

'Wait!' I said outside the cafe. I was scrabbling in strange desperation for my sunglasses. It had stopped raining, the footpath glared, the air was again thin and bright.

The hallway at home was stuffy.

'That you love?' I chose not to answer. I could still hear his car at the end of our road.

'Let-ter!' She must be lying down because of the heat . . . There was a manila envelope waiting for me under the jardiniere. O.H.M.S. My posting had come. Grades 3 and 4, Yardoo Primary.

It is raining now, steady winter rain beating on the hollow of Michael's house. The sound has been creeping up on me ever since the music died. The button glows red on the stereo. Salt dribbles from the empty peanut packet onto the glass table. No Michael.

I leap up from the couch, and hobbling on my numbed left foot as if I'm tethered, open the front door. My car still sits askew on the verge, its wheels streaked with wet country dust. The air is very cold. Stamping my foot to life, I shut the door.

I move swiftly now through every room of Michael's house, opening and closing doors, snapping lights on and off. The rooms are smaller than you think back here. I note in passing an intense disorder. Unmade beds in two rooms. I move on. It is not until I come to the end of the corridor that I know he must be in the music room.

I don't switch on the light. He is sitting on the couch under the window. I go across to him.

He says: 'It's worse when it rains. It's like the whole planet's poisoned.'

Back in the house a phone starts ringing. Lauren? My mother? It doesn't matter. I am moving quite by instinct now.

Travelling

There were four of them who had arrived in Luang Prabang that day, and now hung around the entrance of the Royal Air Lao office in light rain, waiting for a man called Ted Akhito. As far as they could make out (here Ruth for once had made the enquiries, her matric French promoted by Galen), this Ted was a Japanese English teacher who rented rooms to travellers on the second floor. Probably C.I.A. Who wasn't? An introverted, sleuthing silence fell among them, not helped by the rain.

Travellers were scarce in Laos that year, and they seemed to be sticking together, linked by a sort of professional pride. On the traveller's scale of values, Laos had an off-beat, quietly dangerous chic. Vietnam had lost its glamour even for the foolhardy, but in those days, Laos, with war flickering through its jungles so you had to town-hop in a battered DC3, and sleep in the curfew to the distant sound of planes and even gunfire, still had that nice edge of controllable adventure.

In Ban-Houei-Sai, the little border town on the Laotian side of the Mekong, shopkeepers had refused to serve them, and the one cafe that would give them a meal had been full of armed soldiers and beefy American men in laundered mufti. *The place is crawling with C.I.A.,* Galen wrote to a friend back in Australia (he liked to write on-the-spot accounts in cafes), *it's probably only a matter of time before the borders are closed.* There was that Shangri-la savour of a soon-to-be-lost frontier.

But last night in Ban-Houei-Sai, while Ruth was dousing herself in a mandi bath, an unseen watcher had laughed at her from behind the window bars. There are peeping Toms everywhere, as Galen said, but there was something about the sureness and scorn of that laugh, its pause, its continuation, as she had clutched a sarong about her pink body and fled down the curfew-darkened corridors of the hotel, that she related to war. She wasn't sure that they had any right to be in this country at all.

It was nearly dark when Ted Akhito arrived, under a dripping umbrella. They followed him up a staircase that opened, loft-like, into a large rectangular room with shuttered windows at either end. It was bare except for the rows of bamboo mats along the walls.

'Five hundred kip a night', said Ted Akhito, looking at his watch. He was young, as young as they were, dressed in Westernised tropical whites. There was no question of bargaining about the price.

'I must go now, I have a class. I'll be back later to check things out. Curfew is at ten o'clock.' He spoke excellent English without an accent, except he said 'class' like an American. What was he doing in Luang Prabang? Yes, almost certainly C.I.A.

Mats were already being claimed while he was talking.

'Here?' said Ruth to Galen. There were two mats together near the staircase. That tiny panic, like schooldays, when the gym teacher would say, 'Find yourself a spot', and you'd jostle and circle to be at the back, near a friend. Galen shrugged. She took the mat that would be furthest from Bob, the Englishman, who as usual was hovering to see what Galen would do.

The Canadian was already striding up and down the room, looking out the windows.

'Wonder where you can get a meal in this town', he said.

'Wouldn't mind a cup of tea', said Bob. He was always ready to attach himself to a superior energy.

Galen was flicking through his *Student's Guide to South-East Asia*. 'Got the name of a cafe here somewhere', he said.

There was a general movement to the stairs.

'Hold on', Bob was muttering, arm-deep in his ruck-sack. 'I've lost my mac.'

Ruth hurried to join Galen, who with Canada was already at the bottom of the stairs.

Luang Prabang's wet empty streets did not seem under seige. The *Student's Guide* was pre-war, but the Melody Café still existed by the river, a dimly-lit little cave scattered with a handful of their own kind. A hang-out. Like the German Dairy in Chieng-Mai, or the Thai Song Greet in Bangkok. Made you realise that the trail had been well and truly blazed before you. Look at the menu. Along with all the usual rice and noodles, you could get roles and jam for breakfast, bolled eggs, stek fry, bananas milkshek. They wouldn't be quite the real thing of course, they were hybrid dishes cooked up for nostalgic Western palates.

'I'm gonna have me a steak', Canada announced soon after they had settled themselves around a table.

'Steak!' said Bob, looking at the menu. 'That's eight hundred kip. It's a rip-off.'

Canada slapped the table lightly.

'This is a rip-off, that's a rip-off, *oh* you're having *steak, I* haven't had steak since I left home.' He addressed the table in general. He was never personal. He went on. 'Why are travellers so god-damned *mean?* Like it's immoral to spend money or something. They haggle over anything to save five lousy cents. Me, if I want steak, I'll *have* steak.'

'All very well if you've got the money', said Bob, still staring at the menu.

Ruth tried to catch Galen's eye. A taboo had been broken. They had been so conscientious about adopting the right ethos. If you let them rip you off they didn't respect you, and you were spoiling it for those who came after you. The less you spent, the more you roughed it, the better traveller you were. For some it was not just economical, it was spiritual. Working off some of that bad European karma, vaguely evening up the score. 'We lived just like the villagers.' After India, there were some travellers who never used knives and forks, or a handkerchief, or a sit-down toilet again.

Canada was untroubled by the niceties of the sub-culture. He didn't look like the typical traveller either. Western males in Asia seemed to become feminised. Like Galen or Bob, or the travellers at the other tables, their muscles became wasted from dysentery, their bodies were lost within their own over-sized clothes. Their hair grew, they adopted bangles or earrings or headscarves, their gestures were smaller, guarding their own space. Canada's denim shorts were tight around well-built thighs. He wore a heavy leather belt around his hips. He was square-featured and tanned like an old-time football star. The exchange of names didn't interest him. He called everyone 'Hey', they called him Canada.

The cafe-owner's wife stood before them, smiling. Young, very upright and finely attentive though a child was hovering by her thigh. A grandmother held a baby, and an older child played around the kitchen door. They smiled at her as they gave their orders. Except Bob. He was deliberating over the omelette or the fried eggs.

'Excuse me, excuse me', he called out after her as she had turned towards the kitchen. Again she stood before them.

'Look, do you mind, I'll have the boiled eggs instead, two soft boiled eggs, two minutes each, understand? Two minutes.' He held up two fingers and tapped his watch. She nodded.

'Thank you so very much', said Bob. He treated her to one of his weary smiles.

Ruth kept her head turned away as Bob subsided, satisfied, on the bench next to her. When they had first met Bob, in the German Dairy, a week and a country ago, she had not been sure whether in these transactions he wasn't trying to produce a comedy turn. He looked as if he was going to be funny, with all those schoolboy freckles and his hair barbered ruthlessly above his ears. He drank milkshakes for his health, he told them, by way of introduction, and his smile seemed benignly goofy under his milk-speckled moustache. Hepatitis, caught in India. Infinitely travel-worn, like all those emerging from the great sub-continent.

Like her, he couldn't seem to get the hang of foreign

currency. 'This . . can't . . be . . right', he had said to the German Dairy's proprietor. 'I . . will . . not . . pay . . so . . much.' He spoke in pained, deliberate tones, shaking his head slowly for emphasis. Galen had stepped in, and sorted it out for him. But he'd still felt aggrieved as he walked back with them to their hotel. Ruth's old hope, half forgotten in the serious business of travelling, of finding a fellow clown, died. He wasn't trying to be funny. It was a form of tantrum they were to see every time he had to part with his money.

'Nice place', Ruth said to Galen, across the table. Galen didn't answer. He and Canada were picking their way through an abandoned Laotian newspaper, testing out their French.

'I thought you guys were supposed to be bilingual', Galen was saying, laughing.

Their waitress brought them a pot of tea. Galen and Canada looked up, paused, motors idling over. Her swift fingers setting out the cups, her oval face . . .

'They take their time', Bob muttered. 'I'm starving.' He reached a white freckled arm across her to pour himself a cup of tea.

Ruth's legs felt heavy as she crossed them. For a moment she thought of saying to Bob, 'Do you ever feel like you're an inferior physical species?' Like her, Bob was noticeably of Anglo-Saxon stock. Fair skin inclined to flush up in the heat. Blue eyes often sweat-stung. Beige teeth. Innocent knobbly white feet sprawling across thongs. But this was way beyond acceptable perimeters. *Too personal.* The sort of comment she used to make over wine at her own table, safe in that acknowledged femininity that she seemed to have left back in the West.

Was that what she meant? She felt she'd lost a whole persona somewhere along the trail. Become a mere trudging mate whom nobody seemed to hear. It wasn't just that mascara streaked down your face in the humidity and long hair was out of the question, you just tucked it back as best you could. She hated to catch sight of herself in shop mirrors. A large girl with a bare earnest face. Sexless as a missionary. And fat. Getting fatter. There were no shadows, no roles, no corners to hide in anywhere. Just the fact of yourself coming to meet you border after border.

'The women in these parts are supposed to be the most beautiful in the world', Canada said to Galen. His steak had arrived. He was feeling convivial. 'Good grub heh?'

'I wish I knew', said Bob. His eggs had not appeared.

'It pays to order what they know', Canada said, 'if you're hungry'. His eyes glittered at Bob above his busy jaw.

Ruth finished first. Galen worked slowly through his rice, his chopsticks moving in a ruminative way like the fingers of women crouched on doorsteps, searching through their children's hair. Galen had applied himself to the art of chopsticks as he did to everything, with the natural expectation of success.

Ruth preferred to use a fork. The way you could scoop and order and round up with your aggressive Western prongs. And the fork gave her more contact with the food somehow. Sometimes she felt that the closest relationship she had these days was with the plate of food in front of her.

'Ah here we are', Bob was saying, clearing his spot on the table. The eggs had arrived, lolling in a soup bowl. 'Not quite the usual presentation', he had to add, but cheerfully enough, holding one down and tapping around its crown. He smoothed his moustache back, his spoon dived and was dropped clattering onto the table.

'Bloody concrete', he said, reddening under his freckles. The eggs were both hard-boiled.

'He's infantile. It's embarrassing. It's so . . . *colonial.*' Ruth nudged Galen aside on the walk back to the hotel to share her anger with him in the dark. Bob had stood up in the cafe, waving his eggs at their waitress, calling out 'Look here'. They had left him personally supervising the timing of two more eggs in the kitchen.

'Well', said Galen. 'So what?' He kept walking fast to catch up with Canada.

'I'm fed up with him. We've had him hanging round us since Chieng Mai.'

'Oh God', said Galen. 'Chaos in Laos.'

'Oh very clever.'

'Honestly', said Galen, 'when are you just going to shut

up and enjoy yourself like everybody else?'

'Don't lecture me', cried Ruth. She wheeled off and sat on the steps of a building they were passing.

'I'm going on', said Galen. She saw him meet up with Canada at the next corner and, both hunched over with hands in pockets, disappear into the shadows of the long avenue.

Ruth didn't sit there for long. The flap of a single pair of thongs was fast approaching. Like her, Bob had no sense of direction, and hated walking alone in the dark.

Back at Ted Akhito's, there was an hour left to them before curfew, but it was not inviting. A naked bulb hanging in the middle of the dormitory cast a subdued, yellowish light. Canada and Galen were making rapid male preparations for sleep. There was a flash of Galen's long hopping white legs, before he was magically prone, sheathed and flattened. It would have been indecent to watch Canada as he thrashed and muttered his way into his sleeping-bag and turned his face to the wall.

Galen re-surfaced. He lay half out of his bag, trying to read *Anna Karenin;* he maintained that he could not fall asleep without a dose of the printed word, but in this light he had to run his fingers under the lines like a ritual of prayer. Perhaps it was a gesture of waiting for Ruth. At home she always fell asleep to Galen's lamp and the soft turning of pages. She would have leaned across him, and said 'Where are you up to?' *Anna Karenin* was her book: she had read it for four whole days in the hold of an Indonesian cargo boat. She had been carried along by the book as much as by the boat, the story had unfolded to the rise and drop of the seas. Nineteenth century Russia would always be associated with the dazed hustle of their arrival in Djakarta.

Bob came panting up the stairs.

'There's not a soul to be seen out there. Do you think it's a sort of pre-battle hush?' He spoke loudly, as if he were rejoining a party.

'The light!' growled Canada from his corner. 'D'ya need that light?'

‘All right, all right’, said Bob, ‘it isn’t curfew yet’. He lingered at the end of Galen’s mat, ready to conspire. But Ruth had turned to unpack, and Galen was closing his book.

‘Christ I’m tired’, said Bob. He flapped across the room to the door. They heard a hiss, ‘Where’s the ruddy switch?’ and the light went out.

Ruth was left crouching by her pack, unresolved. Galen was still. She had intended to unpack, shake out her hair, write in her diary, all without reference to Galen, but within his range of observation: it would have been a wordless interaction that brought them to the conclusion of this day, and the battle between them that each day’s travelling seemed to bring. Then one of them might have been ready to make a sign, that across these strange deprivations, their unity survived.

Darkness had pre-empted her. She was now a mere night scuffler. She moved like a thief, each sound was a betrayal. Unlayer her pack. Possessions as familiar as her hands. Book, sarong, diary, toothbrush. The layers descended in relevance. Right at the bottom, occasionally disturbed by the hands of customs officers, was a woollen sweater still smelling of home, and the photos of her family.

On the other side of Galen, Bob was crackling out his sleeping-bag. It was covered in a crisp papery plastic. For lightness. They had heard a lot about that bag. How it had been specially made for walking tours in Wales. Double thickness down, much too hot for Asia, with complicated aerations, all zip-controlled. Rolled up to the size of a giant green salami. A room-mate, French, had tried to rip it off in Calcutta.

Zip, crackle, deep sighs from Bob, more zips, more sighs. A final crackle. Enough to make the back of your skull crawl, Bob’s horny feet manipulating plastic.

Galen had yawned, was turning over. Now to inch her way into her sleeping-bag, lay back her head. The big windows let in a grey translucence that had settled over the room. The night outside was silent. *You’d hardly know there was a war on,* she would write to her parents when they were safely out of Laos. She wrote them hasty air-letters of cool-minded reportage, casual feats of endurance. My goodness, they would write back, you have to be young!

Beside her, Galen had started moving, in a series of subtle, strait-jacketed shrugs. Ruth listened, and understood. He was taking off his passport pouch and money belt, and kicking them to his feet. 'Trust nobody', they had been told. She shut her eyes. For yet another night, they were to lie side by side like brother and sister, burdened with old knowledge of each other. Galen, her husband for nearly half a year, had become a traveller, a different person to her. But he remained after all, like her, a well-warned child of the bourgeoisie. She turned over then, ready to sleep.

'Look after her', Galen's father had said. Of course he hadn't had a tea-towel over one shoulder, down on the wharf, he was wearing his suit as he did whenever he left the farm, but that was how she saw him. Waving them off with a floury hand.

Every time Galen had taken her home, Norman would make scones. Rubbed butter into flour with trembling old brown hands. Cut the dough with an upturned sherry glass, up and down, swift as a process worker. 'Open the oven door for me darling', he would say to Galen. Out the kitchen window, just beyond the chook sheds, you could see the bare brick walls of suburban houses. The poultry farm was in an outer suburb now. There had been nothing but bush and market gardens when Norman bought the place, and flatness, a convex landscape after England, Galen said. He'd been twelve. His mother died that year. He always called his home 'the farm'.

It took him an hour by bus to get to uni. He was always late for morning lectures. When she first knew him, he used to disappear mysteriously from pubs or parties. Slipping off to catch the last bus home. He got a lot of work done that way, he said.

Meeting Norman that first time, she'd been a bit breathy and overdone. She used to think she had to keep Galen entertained. She'd admired the scones, admired Norman's history book collection, pranced around the sheds and admired the chooks. Smoked like a chimney, dropping ash in her tea, but you couldn't do anything wrong in Norman's kitchen. As they were leaving (they were going to a party in Ruth's mother's Mini, Galen at the wheel), Norman had said then 'Look after her Galen'. Galen never answered.

In the humidity, Galen's face was very sallow. The acne scars across his jaw seemed to darken, reminders of an old battle. Now that he was so thin, he looked more like his father. Like this, from the side, his head bowed over the letter he was writing on his knee. She watched a tear of sweat escape his headband and linger in the hollow of his cheek. She could never imagine Galen with his mother. He seemed to spring straight from the mother and father both in Norman.

'Looks like rain', Bob said.

They were sitting in the courtyard of a monastery, half-way up the hill overlooking the town. It didn't look like they would get much further. They were sated, even by the rich smells that hung in the humidity, of dung and damp undergrowth, and rotting overripe fruit. Even Canada, having paced the circumference of the courtyard, was sitting down now, smoking, over by the gate.

That morning, their pace had quickened with the promise and strangeness of a new place. Luang Prabang, after a night's sleep, was a beautiful country town. There were red blossoming trees along roads that still gleamed from last night's rain. High above the town, a golden dome shone from a hilltop, like a fairytale turret. Townspeople smiled at them, curiously. They shared cigarettes and sign-language with a group of soft-faced, schoolboy monks. This was how they liked to be received, as a species of scruffy pilgrim.

'Stomach's feeling strange', said Bob. 'Think I'm in for another attack of the runs.'

Galen wrote on, rapidly. *I am sitting on the steps of a tenth century drinking-fountain,* she read at the top of his page, *in thirty-five degree humidity.* Facts she hadn't been aware of.

A bell had rung and the monks had disappeared. The sky

that hung before them over the town was now a luminous grey. Palm trees in the courtyard started to rustle and wave. Nobody else seemed to be around.

Canada stubbed out his cigarette and started back down the hill.

'Coming?' said Bob to Galen.

The four of them moved towards the town like an awkward beast whose legs wished to go different ways. Canada was off-hand, accompanying them this morning as if there were nothing better to do. He walked ahead, restlessly peering into door-ways of the ochre-coloured buildings, disappearing up alleys, looking for action. His presence made Ruth uneasy.

She was used to travelling at Galen's pace. He always had an air of elation about him, discovering new territory. He loved to plan their route, and fit together the puzzle of map and reality. His passport pouch swung out and back to its bay within his hollow ribcage. The tails of the black and white scarf he wore as a headband flew out behind him. Travelling was a feast of the eye, he said. Was there such a state as pure vision?

While she trailed, glimpsing the backdrop through a web of thoughts. Like watching ants as a child, guessing at purpose and connection in a teaming other world. Distanced by the huge eye of the self.

Sometimes she found herself silently in step with Bob. He always seemed to be holding his words in check, until he caught up with Galen. Bumping together, they didn't even bother to say sorry.

'Ouch', said Galen suddenly. She had walked into him and trodden on one of his thongs. He held it up by one dangling tentacle.

'Sorry', Ruth said. Galen was very attached to those thongs. His Bangkok thongs. He called them art objects. The crinkled rubber was printed with a series of red and green music notes, gay inconsequential crochets and quavers, worn away now to the hills and valleys of his feet.

'Damn', he said. His eyes, looking at her, were as dark as the black checks in his scarf. *'Why can't you keep up with me?'*

The rain didn't matter. Running in the rain had been one of her specialities in the old days. Theatrical liberation like moonlight swims and talking for a whole evening in her 'Juliet of the Spirits' voice. Funny, you couldn't see the rain falling. Just the puddles widening, dimpling, somehow connected with the descent of the huge grey sky.

Already the aisles through the market stalls were running miniature rivers, gorges, lakes. She had to hitch up her skirt, pry up each footstep, her shoulder-bag slapping against her hip. Not such a short cut back to the hotel after all. Galen in bare feet would be nearly at the Melody by now. Untrammeled.

Most of the stalls were empty, the mats rolled up where this morning's produce had been laid out. Just a few women under one of the big umbrellas, smoking and laughing. Probably at her, the only person out in the rain. Eyes down, picking her way home as fast as she could. Focus on that emptiness three paces ahead. Do not look at me. Alone, it was always like this.

'Hey', Canada said, appearing at the top of the stairs and turning back to the others. 'D'ya hear about the two German guys? They hired themselves a boat and went downriver. Haven't been seen since.'

'Pathet Lao got 'em I spose', called out Bob. 'Anyone know for sure?'

'Ask Ted Akhito', said Galen, on his way to the dormitory. The others laughed.

Ruth looked up from the mat that defined her territory. It was late afternoon, they had taken what you might call a long lunch. Whenever she was not with them they seemed to come a little closer to the action of the place.

Surprisingly they came and stood around her mat. Galen crouched down beside her. Bob started moving his hands together and apart in a little concertina movement that she had come to recognise. He was shuffling an imaginary pack of cards.

'We've decided to play bridge', he told her.

'I don't play', Ruth said.

The three of them were damp and breathless, seemed to

be sharing a joke. Boyos returning from the pub. Galen put a hand on her shoulder. He was still barefoot.

'Bob's going to teach you. Bob's going to be your partner.'

'You know I hate playing cards', Ruth said to him.

Bob and Canada were already settling themselves around a spare mat under the window.

'Come on', Galen said. 'We'll be nice to you. Promise.'

Bob was dealing.

'You sort them into suits', he said. 'Descending order of value. Ace, King, Queen, Jack — 4, 3, 2, 1.' He was frowning, busy, spitty-sharp. Bob came into his own when he played cards.

The faces on the cards were stern and mediaeval as they spilled out of her hand. Bob went on, about contracts, tricks, trumps.

'What?' she said to Galen.

'Just listen and play', Galen said, not looking up from his own cards. 'You'll pick it up.' That's what he had always done.

On the other side of her, Canada lazily pulled cards in and out of the fan in his hand. He lay on his side, one heavy thigh lapping the other. His eyes had never flickered once in her direction. Why had she let herself be drawn into this? Listen. Keep up. Play.

'Nine clubs', she offered, hopefully.

Bob flung down his cards.

'You haven't been listening, have you? You don't understand.'

Ruth couldn't help the slow smile spreading across her face.

'I can't seem to see the *point* of the game.' She heard Galen begin to laugh.

'Hey', said Canada to Galen. 'How long have you been travelling with this chick?'

Galen couldn't stop laughing. He rolled onto his back and up again, his headband fell across his eyes.

'Oh boy.' He put a hand on Ruth's knee. 'This is for life', he said.

'*Mais où est* Ted Akhito?' Ruth asked the clerk in the Air Lao office again.

'*Ça ne fait rien* Madame, *vous pouvez payer ici'*, came the same reply.

Ruth turned back to the others. 'It's no good. We'll just have to give him the hotel money and hope for the best.'

'Ask for a receipt', said Galen.

'Bloody irresponsible', said Bob, counting out his notes. 'I think we have every right not to pay.' But they had already decided that it would be too risky just to leave the town without somehow paying the mysterious Ted Akhito, whom they had never seen since that first night. He probably had friends in high places.

'Hurry up', said Canada. Outside, the Air Lao cattle truck that ferried passengers between the airport and the town had started up its engine. As before, they were to be its only passengers.

Ruth was the first to sling her bag into the back of the truck. The others hoisted themselves up while she climbed over the boards at the side and swung in. The truck lurched off. They held on to the cabin, standing up.

'All right?' Galen asked Ruth. She nodded.

After their long walk to the Golden Dome, Ruth and Galen had told the others that they would be leaving Luang Prabang the next day. Bob said it was funny, but he'd been thinking of leaving too. Canada just seemed to be with them as they were buying their tickets. You could get used to a place very quickly, they said, it was always a relief to be moving on.

From the truck they could see behind their street now, to paddy-fields spreading under water, islanded with palm-trees and bamboo huts, dotted with bending, slow-moving figures. The truck was speeding up. Now, in their final glimpse of the town, they could grasp its strictly civic plan, its streets and squares set out under the Golden Dome, the steaming river that curved around it and disappeared into alien hills. Like the two Germans, who had never been found. A flock of camouflage-splattered helicopters rose like smoke in the distance. In those hills and jungles there would be the sort of scenes you see in newsreels at home.

‘Hey!’ Canada was pointing across a square. There, surely, hurrying out of a building, was the neat white figure of Ted Akhito.

‘Well I like *that’,* Bob said. But they were all smiling. They had rightly been judged not to be security risks. They were too lazy. Too cautious. You’d hardly know there was a war on. If you played by the rules.

The town was behind them now, shadowed by its own hills.

Lilies

When Christine Hollins came home she knew what she wanted to do. Find a place in the bush somewhere and talk, properly, with her mother. Then at the airport, in the flat white light she had forgotten, she saw her parents, shrunken, aged, looking anxiously in the wrong direction, and she paused. She felt it was another person who was approaching them.

Her parents now lived in a flat in the Bishop Byatt Retirement Home. But there in the tiny living-room were the Sydney Town prints that used to hang in the rectory hall. And the Persian scatter rug and the green leather wireless chair and the fluted daisy teacups from a thousand parish afternoons. Like her parents, they seemed to have lost authority.

'Well, nice to have you back, Chris', her father said as they settled rather formally around the room.

'She looks tired out', her mother called from the kitchenette.

'You've put on weight', said Helen.

This too was the same. Her family had never been very good at celebrations: gathered together they could only follow the right forms. For years they had done their living in separate rooms while her mother scuttled up corridors with a summons to meals or the telephone. Even Christmas had been a vague affair over a Mills and Ware's pudding, snatched between services, shared with the odd lonely parishioner.

Now they balanced the daisy cups on their laps, nibbled on biscuits. Her father pursed his lips with concentration as he reached for the sugar, stirred, sipped to taste.

'Where are the kids?' Christine asked Helen.

'Back at school, thank God.' Her sister wasn't any more maternal with the years. Or didn't show it. The light cast an almost metallic gleam on her long blonde hair. The line of her black-rimmed eyes was like a wire.

'Another cup?' their mother asked.

Helen stood up. 'Actually, I must be off. I have to see someone before I pick up the kids.' Helen had always slipped off somewhere.

Her mother's cup clicked in its saucer.

'We're dying to hear all about your trip.' She smiled.

The flesh falls away, the colours fade, only the forms remain. Like this featureless room, with so much left out, left behind. Christine looked at her mother, trying to remember, glints, flashes, a distant grace . . . You've willed it away, she thought, but even the anger was an echo. She was suddenly so tired that her mother jumped in and out of focus before her eyes. Crouched in her chair, bending to sip, she was the figure in the front pew who dipped in prayer . . .

Within a week Christine had found her shack in the hills and was gone.

Violet Hollins came down with flu at the end of summer. Nothing dramatic, but it left her coughing weakly in bed for nearly a month, and by winter had become a way of life in the flat. John Hollins stayed cheerful, cooked their evening chops, and thanked everybody at the Bishop Byatt for their kind invitations which Violet kept on refusing.

Her daughters visited her. She dressed then and shuffled into the living-room in a cardigan buttoned askew. She sat with her head shaking slightly, leaning forward when they spoke as if following the lines of a play.

'I must bring the kids over. That is, when they can fit it in.' Helen rolled her eyes, but added: 'They've been asking to see Gran'.

Christine saw that Helen, in her own way, was as touched

and guilty as she was. They made the tea now, moving gently round their mother. They offered her shopping trips, drives, films. She shook her head, smiling. But when they got up to go, she followed them to the door.

'Now what was it?' Her hands smoothed her thighs where an apron used to lie. 'There was something I was going to tell you . . .'

It's too late, Christine thought as she drove home.

Then one afternoon she arrived at the flat, knocked, called out, let herself in. She found her mother sitting in the grey light of her bedroom. She did not seem to notice as Christine pulled up a chair in front of her. They were silent while outside, rain trickled from the gutters.

'Hey Mum.' Christine spoke out of the terror of the last few moments, that she no longer existed for her mother, had denied her and lost her for good. 'Listen, why don't you come and spend a few days with me?' Her mother turned to her with unaccusing eyes.

'A change of air would do you good. Come on, I'll help you pack.' She would not allow her mother to refuse. This was suddenly the right time for them both.

Violet nodded slowly and stood up. She looked around her. 'I'd better leave a note for Daddy', she said.

Christine drove fast through late afternoon traffic. Was she overdoing things again? There was no electricity at the shack, and the nights were freezing. Would her mother even notice where she was? Then, crossing the Causeway, she was suddenly between two realities. She had done this before, or dreamt it, crossed a river into fading light, her mother beside her, taking her home. Where had she seen it? In London, before she had decided to come back? She hummed a little into the silence of the car as they sped up into the hills.

Violet noticed that a change came over Christine as she guided the car down the long rutted driveway to her shack.

'There's Jesse barking! He hears me coming way back on the road.' Her voice was eager.

They pulled up, scattering hens, amongst old sheds and rusting farm machinery.

Violet straightened up beside the car. In the half light two ducks watched her, very white, solid and grave in the long green grass. A foxy dog danced behind a gate. The air against her cheeks was cold.

'Looks like we're in for another frost tonight.' Christine had opened the gate, was hugging the ecstatic dog against her chest. Violet followed her across the yard. They paused on the verandah.

'How do you like my view?'

Beyond the yard, green pasture fell into a valley, disappeared into a line of trees and rose again to meet the sky that arched above them.

'It's so quiet.'

'I might be a hundred miles out, here.'

'Don't you get nervous?'

'Jesse's my protector, aren't you boy? Come on, it's getting dark.' She crossed the creaking verandah and unpadlocked the door.

The last light shone through a four-paned window into a dim kitchen. Christine lit kindling waiting in a wood stove and set a gas lamp on the table.

'Make yourself at home, I'll just shut up the chooks.'

Violet heard her voice calling, young and echoing, out in the darkness. The gas lamp hissed softly. Light swayed up on the ceiling. Beyond its circle were dark shapes and corners. She sat very still at the table.

'It reminds me of a time . . . do you remember Casson?' They were sitting over empty plates, the lamp between them.

'The rectory by the river and swimming off a boat and some boys we used to play with all the time . . .?' Christine leaned over and topped up Violet's glass.

'The Spences. So you remember them? You must have been, what, five or six when we came back to the city?'

'Yes, but the country made a big impression on me.' For some reason her memories of that time were speared with sadness, twilight over the river, low rocky hills around the town that threatened her, a sort of Sunday night feeling of being lost and alone.

'Of course we had electricity, but we had a wood stove and it was very quiet like this.'

'What happened to the Spences?'

'They went to Melbourne after Casson and we never saw them again. Just Christmas cards. I haven't thought of them for ages.' Violet looked across Christine to the forgotten life of a fire.

'You know', Christine said, watching her, 'you and Dad could easily find a little place around here. There are plenty if you look, and they're quite cheap and comfortable.'

'Oh we couldn't possibly. Dad isn't a country person. And he loves the Home.'

'What about you? You haven't looked exactly happy recently.'

'Haven't I dear? Convalescent blues.' Violet put down her glass.

Christine leaned forward, flushed from the fire and wine.

'Come on Mum, don't give me that. Are you going to stay a convalescent for the rest of your life? How can you bear it, living in that place, all ping-pong and sing-song and isn't it nice? Why have you just given up like this?'

'Oh Chris.' Violet waved a hand in front of her eyes. 'No dear, don't, you don't understand. It's all right there really, it's not much different from before. It's me, I'm tired, I have to catch up . . . somewhere . . .' Her head had started shaking again.

Christine stood up and put on the kettle, closed her eyes against the fire. What had she done? What did she know after all? Their lives were so different. She slumped into the chair by the stove, her hands searching out Jesse's back.

Violet was sitting very still, letting her heart beat out its panic. It passed more quickly then. The darkness. The light actually seemed to dim. Lately it had been happening more often, triggered off by the phone ringing, a moment's indecision in the supermarket, a cat calling in the night. As if the darkness was gathering all around her, waiting for her to forget that she had ever been alive at all.

It was quiet again. There was the lamp, the fire. It always left her clearer for a little afterwards, the mind unrolled itself, even and sure. She was almost grateful to it.

Back at the Home, no it had started years before, she and her mind often seemed to have come apart. Couldn't remember what she'd got up for in the morning, and then what to do after that. Until she just had to trust to her body's long habit of living to do it for her. Always feeling there was something she had to remember, something vital, for which she needed time and quiet. There wasn't much of that at the Home. 'Keeping busy', they all said that when they asked after each other in the courtyard. What had Chris said, that it was a silly place where they played ping-pong? But they knew that, all of them. Keeping busy: it was a sort of motto of the place. Her last parish.

And there was Chris, looking miserable. Poor old Chris, she had meant to help, she had always been like that, running to you bursting over with an idea about this or that, or something she'd made for you, and the next moment in tears, stamping her foot, and you didn't know where you'd gone wrong, where you'd let her down. John understood Chris better, that she had to try things, she had to battle with her own nature all the time. You didn't see it in John, but he was a battler too, hours in his study, praying, reading, coming out quiet and cheerful again, a conclusion reached, food for next week's sermon. You had to respect him for it, but it was lonely in the beginning outside his door, part of the world that had to be forgiven.

Christine had inherited it somehow, this drive to saintliness. Along with his high forehead, his short strong limbs. But it had been hard for her to find her way. Was this it here, alone? In workman's boots and those rings studded up her ears? And what about Helen, always smiling through her hair . . .?

My daughters are strangers to me. She sometimes said that to herself to try and work it out. Because this couldn't be the whole story, the way they looked at her sometimes with hard grown-up faces that made her nervous. If she could get past all those little phrases, 'doing nicely', 'going through a phase', 'happily settled down', now 'got their own lives to lead' — the words you use for other people, like a currency across the years — if she could get back to them, Helen and Christine, two heads, one blonde, one brown, bent over the kitchen table, quarrelling over coloured pencils, there was a knowledge there, there must be, that could show you what they had become.

'Why do you live here Chris?' She had never asked her before. She had accepted it as part of the world's drawing away.

'I'm nearly thirty.' Christine turned to her, reached for her wine. 'I knew I wanted a place of my own back in England, in the end. I wanted to grow things. I don't know why. I found I like looking after things.' She said this almost defiantly. My dog, my chooks, my ducks. Two goats arriving next week. My goats. Jealous even that the cows her landlord ran on the place were not her own. An orgy of ownership, of care. Even of this shack, that she was saving up to buy, scrubbing the old lino, blacking the stove, oiling the flywire door. She looked after it like a baby.

'And what about those photos over there?' Violet pointed to a fan-like arrangement pinned to the back of the kitchen door.

'They were all taken during my time with the Youth Centre in London.' Christine got up and went over to them. Violet joined her.

'That's me with Eugene Hoffman outside the Centre, we ran it together, that's Eugene playing basket-ball with some of the boys, that's our Christmas party, what a riot, that's the group of kids we took to the Lake District.'

Eugene Hoffman featured in every shot, a thin blonde young man dressed like a fisherman in a poloneck sweater and beanie. It was his face in the blown-up photo in the centre, caught turning to a call, beginning a smile that deepened his long jaw, eyes searching out the caller, deepening and disappearing into a maze of printed dots.

'Who was he?'

'An American, from Baltimore, ex-priest, social worker, teacher, traveller.'

'Did you get to know him well?'

'We lived together, more or less.' In sleeping-bags, above the Youth Centre, breakfasts by the tea-urn, wearing coats and gloves, planning the day over a trestle table. Knowing at the time she was serving her essential apprenticeship.

'What was there between you?'

'He was the man of my life.' It was good to say it to her mother, even if it gave the wrong impression. She had always known it was possible for a human being to be like that. She had found him and he had taken her along with him. Work, ideas, laughter, work, it had been like suddenly mastering an instrument, or she was the instrument, no straining, no false notes. It had seemed easy then.

'What happened?' Did he treat her well, did he make her happy as I could never do?

'His mother was sick and he had to go back to America.' She thought too that he sensed his time in London was over, his work was done. Too many people depended on him, it was time for them to go on alone. He was telling her then, it was no good, her hand on his arm. He had said: 'If it was to be anyone, it would have been you'. She had tried for a while, had the presumption to try to live like him. But love for her had to be through her hands, in what she touched and held and was given back.

'So that's it?' Her mother would never understand.

'Oh there are letters. He says he'd like to come to Australia one of these days. But yes, that's it. And there'll never be anyone else.'

Violet was silent. She would have liked to offer comfort, denial, you are so young, how can you know . . . but they were easy words against Christine's face, this kitchen. Hadn't she too once held on to such an ending, at Casson, when she was in love, with Jim, Jim Spence?

Christine was clearing their plates off the table. 'Ready for bed?'

It was all here waiting for her to put together, to find under layers of living. It musn't slip away again, the man in the kitchen, the woman by the fire.

'Coming?' asked Christine, picking up the lamp.

She followed her daughter into the other room.

Morning revealed a foreign country outside the window, mists rolling away from silver fields.

'Did you see the frost we had last night?' Christine asked as she stoked the fire. 'I hope you were warm enough.'

'Oh yes. The best sleep I've had for a long time.' The night had done its work for Violet. She had slept heavily, moving in and out of dreams she had forgotten, but which brought her straight back to the morning, ready.

'I must be off', said Christine, pulling on her boots. She taught three days a week at the local high school. 'I'll be back about four. You can keep the fire going, I've chopped some more wood.' She had not slept well, aware of her mother's presence across the room. She wished she had not spoken of Eugene last night.

Violet nodded at her. Christine had never been very sociable in the morning. But Christine lingered. 'You'll be all right here won't you? Why don't you go for a walk? There's some arum lilies growing down by the creek. You've always liked those lilies, haven't you?'

Yes, yes, go! You don't know what it is you are offering me. Violet sat listening as the car engine turned over and died, once, twice and then away, steaming, bumping up the drive.

It had been a larger room than this, a real old rectory kitchen, but the light was the same, the bright innocent sky over the sink, the floor dappled from trees outside the verandah. One bulb above the table. None of the spotlights and stainless steel of modern kitchens, everything concealed. A pile of wood by the stove, a box of oranges wedged into a corner. The heat and cold and blowflies rushing in the door.

Another era. Life at walking pace. Radio serials, Mother's Union meetings, children's voices down at the river all through the long afternoons. No trouble with falling congregations then, everybody came to church on Sunday.

It was their first parish. They were very busy. They tried very hard. John with his painstaking sermons, his visits to all the farms, even the shacks in the hills. And she, with fêtes and socials and afternoon teas, let alone two small children. The kitchen was her scene of battle, her introduction to the mysterious ways of things. Of Things. To this day, a pot burned if she turned her back, backs and fronts joined together if she sewed on a button, her sewing machine would only go if she hummed and looked out the window and pretended she didn't care. But then she had wondered how she would ever keep the household creaking over from day to day. How long would the women of the parish forgive a no longer new bride for her misshapen pikelets, her husband's creased cassock, the curtains that hung unhemmed in the rectory lounge-room? She felt their eyes on her in that kitchen, sweating, prodding, stirring her lumpy gravy over a copy of *Golden Wattle,* pouring her unjelled jam down the drain at the back steps. It was like a revenge, she used to think, by all domestic objects around her, for having ignored them up till then, reading a book in her grandmother's house, being looked after.

And yet it was in the kitchen, making one of her uncertain cups of tea, too strong, more water, too weak, if I give it a stir . . . that she first noticed Jim Spence looking at her, laughing. He'd taken to dropping in at odd hours, always just seemed to miss John, and would sit watching her blunders as if he enjoyed them. One day he took her hands as she wrung them and said: 'You're like a little girl. Don't ever grow up.' Watching her, smiling as she blushed. It hadn't occurred to her that her struggles could be funny, could even be endearing. It was as if she had moved onto a stage. It was irresistible.

Had she thought much about him before this attention, as apart from Dot and Jim Spence, one of those couples on bank postings, who came and went, and remained outsiders? But Jim Spence had been to school with John. 'Wonderful to find you here', he said, and presuming friendship, took them over for the summer. 'Old Happy Hollins', Jim called John. He didn't seem to take it seriously, that John was now the rector of the local church.

'What do you do for Saturday lunch? Right, how about a picnic by the river?'

'Dot says she's just baked a cake, what if we walk over after tea?'

'You mean you play bridge, then we've got a four!'

'We're used to moving about in this job', Dot confided to her over the dishes. 'We settle in quickly wherever we go.'

They sought out the Hollins daily, as if they needed them. Picnics drifted on to dinner: night after night they put the children to bed, sat on the rectory verandah, drinking beer, swatting mosquitoes. The children formed a foursome of their own. She could see her two little girls slick-haired like seals, squealing as the two Spence boys bombed them from over-hanging branches into the dark green water. Dot quickly saw that Vi needed a hand. She rushed out and brought in her washing if the dust was blowing, took over her kitchen for the dreaded annual cake stall. Twelve blowaway sponges that you practically had to hold down, and the benches clear. ('I wash as I go', said Dot, elbows up at the sink, setting up a sort of rhythm, like a jazz musician.)

John and she accepted it, this brief take-over: they didn't know what else to do. They were used to accommodating people, fitting their life around others' needs. And it intrigued them a little, a breath from the easy frivolous world that had always passed them by. They muttered protests about sermons and Sunday school, but it was summer, the whole town slowed down to the pace of a ball tossed in an idle game of tennis. They rather enjoyed for a while being Happy and Vi making mistakes over the bridge table.

Dot and Jim were strikingly oddly-matched. Jim was short and slim with heavy brown eyes, straight black hair. He made you think of cricketers, Errol Flynn, or an officer on a British cruise ship. He had an eager, interested air about him, liked to yarn in the pub, make irreverent comments over a few beers. He was, by anybody's standards, a heart-throb in his tennis whites. While Dot looked more like a Girl Guide leader, broad in the beam, sporty calved, hair clipped back off her face. That face, she could see it now, clearer than Jim's, the downward slope of the eyes and mouth, the mole with the hair on the upper lip that seemed to say 'Trust me' as she leaned forward over her knitting, talking. A great talker, talked as rapidly as her hands moved, accounts detailed down to the last minute, the last penny, the last second cousin. She listened too, her eyes were alert, she noticed and could stay silent. She was everybody's mother, good old Dot, she remembered the tomato sauce and the towels, gave the signals of departure. 'Well come on Jimmy', she would say, gathering possessions. 'What, are you tired?' Jim would say, looking round for an unfinished bottle. Until she would touch his arm. 'Please. Home.' And he would get up not looking at her.

You couldn't help wondering what had drawn them together. 'She's a nice girl', John said. 'A stable influence. Spence was a pretty rowdy type at school.' She sensed that John didn't have much serious time for Jim. He listened to his war stories, his cynical stances about farmers and bankers, and said very little. But John never talked about other people. She was alone with her fascination from the start.

For yes, though she didn't have the words to name her feeling, she had noticed Jim Spence, turned to watch him, as probably many women did. She gave herself up to watching him, in his old army fatigues, brown arms emerging from khaki, coaxing up their barbecue fire, neat as an Arab on his heels, quick, skilful, male. When he smiled at her it was as if she had been chosen. His glamour spread to Dot, his children, all of them, until there was a sort of hectic shimmer over the lamp-lit verandah, the dusty tennis courts, the shaded, sluggish river.

Jim Spence catches her eye across the table, brushes her arm as they walk home, feeding tired children witticisms for one another's ears. Appears at her kitchen at dusk to smile at her by her stove, until she feels she can do no wrong. Until she wills it, he opens the gate of their front garden as if she had sent for him, she is there watering the McCartney rose in the summer night. He comes straight to her as he should, she is waiting like all the heroines in all those novels she read in her grandmother's house. Except meanwhile John is putting the children to bed.

You can remember humiliation too. Here she was, an old woman in a dressing-gown, deciding she must dress, pulling yesterday's clammy clothes over her stiff body; this body that once seemed beautiful to her because he said it was. And she, brought up to distrust beauty, to think of herself as a soul without a body, now swivelled on long-tendoned ankles down the main street, dazzled the baker with her Monday morning smile. And pitied poor Dot her hairy calves as they dabbled their feet in the river together. Even then she had suspected that for this, time, if nothing else, would make her pay.

And she had sometimes wondered if the others noticed! That night, towards the end, when Jim had said he fancied a walk. Any takers? They had left her to say shyly she would go. Exultant children, their quick footsteps passed the bright verandahs of the other houses, to stop in the shadows where the street lights finished and make their declarations. Quick we must go back. Returning too gay and generous to John sunk in a book, while Dot made tea in silence.

And then, sooner than expected, the Spences' new posting comes, they are to leave for Melbourne in a fortnight, they are terribly busy, meet only once or twice more with their friends the Hollins. Summer is over anyway, cooler evenings seem less festive in the rectory lounge-room. Dot knits on with itemised reports of travel preparations. Jim drinks and smokes and doesn't look at Violet. When John begs work, they all stand up together.

Everything falls away. Parish duties slide past her as if her term of office were running out. John, the children, come and go around her. She is waiting, when can she see him, tell him, I am ready, take me with you, take me where I belong. She never leaves her kitchen, but he never comes.

Then their last evening, Helen's birthday party, balloons lurching in the windy twilight, the children's voices querulous in the long rectory garden. Dot is sprinkling bread with hundreds and thousands, talking, and suddenly her voice is thickening, 'the strain of it, always on the go, always having to make new friends, why couldn't we just be a family together?' Shoulders shaking over the sink, just as the children run in demanding their party, voice choking, 'as if I'm not enough', what is Dot saying? That it has happened before, an intense friendship with another couple, Jim's even more intense friendship with the wife? That it will happen again? Too late, Dot blows her nose and is serving up the sausage rolls, the men come in and take up positions round the clamouring table. She cannot even look at him now, and what is Christine, tear-stained from Pip Spence's teasing, whispering in her ear: 'Anyway, I like Daddy better than Mr Spence'.

Everything spoiled, streamers fallen into half-eaten cakes, a jungle of grabbing and shouting, nasty cream-smeared faces. His eyes follow her as he crouches behind his sons. Next day limp-bodied balloons catch at her as she crosses the verandah. They were making an early start, Dot said. He's gone.

A fork scraped a bowl, fat hissed, an egg spread across a pan. Winter clouds moved outside her window, children sat quietly, mysterious angels. Without his eyes none of this existed. Nobody broke the silence around her. John said nothing. She was grateful for the warmth of his back. While the other lay with her, walked with her, watched her, listened to her endless muttered debate. The drive to her days was to their finishing, to leave the children sleeping, John in his study, and walk those darkened roads. Smug lights within the houses, insolent smoke tossing from the chimneys, now she was an outcast, burying herself in the bushes by the river, rocking thigh against calf over her loss.

She grew angry with him, old brown eyes, moony face, the friendly man without any friends, the scoffer at security working his way up the bank, the lover who never followed through. Guilt grew, until Dot's face went with her too. She knew now that her days were also lived in this suspense, must be a series of watchings, yieldings.

Summer was coming. She was weary. When would this double life be finished, would it last as long as the hope that she couldn't after all let die? When could her life be light, self-forgetful again, with the simple pleasures, simple shames of those around her?

Then their time too was over in Casson, they moved to the city, a new parish, the children were now both at school. Shyly she turned to them again, but they brushed past her: they had learnt to be alone. Perhaps she was never to be in step with them again? Her days were filled briskly, sometimes she could even miss the daydreams. How long had it taken for her cells to shed him, five, ten years to have forgotten even to say, I have forgotten him. Until he was felt only as a vague stirring in the blood from time to time, an excitement about the first summer evenings, a dark-eyed man, a garden gate. Now, years later, this room.

Violet looked around her. She was standing in the middle of Christine's kitchen. The fire had gone out. Would Chris be annoyed? It must be well past midday, the sunshine outside was shadowed. She should go for a walk before it rained. At least be able to tell Chris she had seen the lilies.

Jesse jumped up delighted from the verandah and led her as if scenting a trail, across the yard, through the gate. He raced on down the hill, far ahead of her. She took it slowly, the luscious green was unexpectedly gravelly, she had to watch her way. The air smelt fresh, of clover. She would like to leave the whole affair back in the staleness of the kitchen. It was, after all, nothing by today's standards, didn't they call it a 'bit on the side', just to name it then had been shocking enough. Yet she had been ready to lie in the bushes with him, she would have left with him on the next train out of town. It had affected her terribly. She could see that now. Beyond the guilt, which in time she forgot along with its cause.

No, it had left her terrified at where the dreams might take you, the lack of substance they revealed. She would never dare to look again into a shimmer, to follow her own voice again. She was unformed somewhere, a child. Rightness was a conspiracy that others knew about, better to follow the path marked out by John and Gran. If it was narrow, it was clear, forget about the light and shade on either side. And when reminders came that these might still exist, panic closed her eyes.

Her foot turned on a stone, she skidded, waving wildly, landed on all fours. 'Damn it all', said Violet, turning herself back and sitting on her bottom in the middle of the hillside. A huge pale sky moved slowly with its clouds above her. Cows in the next paddock shifted bite by bite. She shut her face and felt the sun and wind lightly upon her face.

This was how I was meant to be. That was what it had been about. With Jim she used to shut that thought away as it turned up like a cat at the door. This was how I was meant to be. An answering smile into the sun, yellowed teeth, porous noses, squinted eyes; answering imperfections. Being yourself until you were drunk with the giggly ease of it and could lie back laughing your silly head off. And then afterwards, the peace that descended, the long sweep of the oars bringing them home, the ripples spreading to the banks, the whole boatload of them blessed.

To have gone on like that, would she now be calling 'Come and get it' over a barbecue, waving plump arms in welcome, a cheerful, ripened self? It would have been bridge and beer and camping holidays: would it have lasted, the recognition between them? They were weak, she and Jim, perhaps had needed the solid buffer of Dot and John. Who had aged better. She still played eighteen holes, Dot said in her card a few Christmases ago. Jim had heart trouble, was having to retire early. Is there a moral quality to ageing? Poor old Jim, she hoped life had not found him out too much.

She ought to have been faithful to it, what there was between them, seen its truth however shallow, instead of turning away in fear. It had existed: it was part of her.

John had kept faith with her all these years. Beyond duty, disappointments. From the very first, as she stood in the pew beside her grandmother, he had insisted on seeing her as virtuous as himself. And she had only ever given him a sisterly rubbing-along.

There was her sin, that she had committed once, smiled upon by her grandmother and her friends, as they helped to fix the veil upon her hair. She had carried arum lilies, though her grandmother thought they were more for a funeral than a wedding. But her mother had carried lilies when she married her grandmother's son. A different affair that, a train and a coronet, the bride's hand resting on the shoulder of the man sitting in front of her. To obey until death, five years later.

My mother is ded, she used to write in her room in her

grandmother's house. Nothing could be deader than ded. Except Dad, who had gone away and left her too. There were only those photos left for her, which she crept in to look at in her grandmother's lounge-room. Gran wouldn't approve somehow, Gran didn't like her mother, she knew it. Her mother had been Catholic and had died so that Edmund went away. Or perhaps she had been one of those who *kicked up her heels, was not quite . . .*: in those photos her face was not quite serious in spite of the hand on the shoulder. What would life have been with such a mother?

She rose stiffly and set off again. She must find those lilies.

Nothing was becoming any clearer. The Lord had his purpose for each and every one of us, John said. Could you say that a death long past had blighted a life, left it with an emptiness somewhere? Discount the years of living, doing . . . She saw herself, an old woman, and behind her, cold rooms in dusty houses, spoiled food, ill-made beds, wilting gardens, the quiet man lonely in prayer. And what about the children, not born out of passion, who had grown up silent, apart from her, as if she too had not been there?

She glimpsed the lilies like a cluster of white birds among the bush of the creek, and pushed her way through to them. There was a boulder by the water to sit on and watch them. She was scratched and shaking, she felt a familiar drumming, was it growing dark already? *No,* she said, holding her head rigid, her hands rubbing the gritty surface of the rock, not here, not yet, there are many ways to look at a life, look now at the lilies. 'Consider the lilies of the field, how they grow.'

Here amongst the dimness of the trees, the water rushing by, was the sort of foreboding of her grandmother's lounge-room, the waxen flowers, the heavy frames high on the mantelpiece, taken down by a shy child's hand. The smile of her mother waiting for her.

She was right to come here. Calmer already. The flowers have thick white flesh. Heartshaped around their powdery stamen. They stand so straight on their ridgy stems, some are almost leaning backwards. They grow in theatrical arrangement, like a band of nuns and brides. There are older flowers amongst them, thin brown stalks waving a pod of seeds.

They will all die in the summer, and reappear next year. They come and they go, they toil not . . . perhaps this would do, this acceptance. Stages in a life. Her mother cut down, she grown old, her daughters in some sort of prime. They come and they go. Helen playing out her blessing before her time was over. She knew her, knew that smart swivel, that smile for someone else's eyes. And Christine. Looking for God, her whole house was a shrine to the man in the photograph.

Violet felt a hush, a prickly rustling, then the sudden rush of rain. She had taken too long to get here, it was nearly dark, she was late. Through the bush, the shack was still there against the sky, it was pouring with rain, it looked thundery, but she must get back. Christine would be waiting.

She ran from the shelter of the trees, started to scramble up the hill, slipping, grabbing, gasping to herself, I must get back.

Christine was sitting on the verandah, with a cup of tea and Jesse by her knee. The clouds were still and heavy, covering the light of the sky. It was going to rain, where was her mother? She would go and find her when she finished her tea. She liked to sit here after teaching, between the house and sky, she was at her most private at these moments.

The headmaster at her school was waiting for an invitation to see her place, he'd said again today. One small cloud detached itself from a larger grouping and seemed to skid in the growing wind, straight towards her. It was going to happen. She was prepared.

She wondered again, if you thought hard enough about somebody, if every lover were really only him, could it be his image that was implanted, his spirit that was passed on? She shivered. She was entering dark territory. She thought, there's an awful arrogance in loving, in trying to harness a whole delicate universe to your own. She would almost like to ask her mother how it might be.

It had started to rain, quite heavily, and standing up, she

could just make out the tiny figure of her mother slowly advancing. She must help her, bring her back. She set off into the rain.

Ask her, ask your mother, struggling up the hill, see if she can tell you somehow, your children are born in forms you never dreamt of, you go on to see them grow up strangers, and yet one day you find them living out your patterns, the patterns rutted across their souls.

Burning Off

Vic and Angela lived right in the town, down by the river. Wes and I lived out a bit, under the hill. As the summer came we spent a lot of evenings sitting out on Vic and Angela's front verandah.

Up at our place, the first that Wes and I had ever shared alone, the darkness seemed to lap around our ankles. The town sprawled out below us, a far-away marquee of lights. But here with Vic and Angela we were deep within a community of sounds. Frogs croaked in the still air by the river, Angela's little sprinkler whip-whipped by the gate. Half a block away Poddy Stratton's T.V. droned under its giant antenna. The girls in the schoolteachers' house behind us sent scraps of laughter echoing across the town.

'I thought they were having a night off', Angela said. 'The big blonde one told me they all wanted to wash their hair.' A few cars went by. Most were turning up to the schoolteachers' house. The teachers were said to be a 'good crowd' this year. They joined in, they were having a ball.

No doubt we were being observed too, sitting there like a flashback in the light of a kerosene lamp hung by the door. There was a campfire smell from the mosquito coils that Angela had lit for each of us. Vic's was too close, he knocked it over reaching for a can. Angela relit it. While Wes kept playing, discreet runs that went nowhere, as if to himself.

Poddy Stratton liked to surprise us. Prowl up the verge so as not to crunch the gravel. 'Hod enough for you?' He'd pause by the gate as if he'd just seen us. Vic raised a can to him, Wes put down his guitar. They worked in Poddy's garage when it was busy. Angela pulled out a spare chair. She'd been in the town almost a year now and no longer asked 'Where's Maxine?' Everybody knew that by this time of the night Maxine Stratton would be under the weather. Poddy went everywhere alone.

Poddy sat forward, legs apart, and fitted his stubby finger through the ring of a can. His pull was vicious, froth ran onto the floor. 'Cheers', said Poddy. We all sat forward a little, in his honour, our visitor.

'Ye-es', said Poddy, as if continuing a conversation, which in a way he was. 'It's gunna be a record summer.' His voice was pitched to reach the end of the verandah. He scanned us with his dark, ringed eyes. Poddy afterhours, shaved jowls and sports shirt sleeves ironed out in right-angles above his biceps, had a headmasterly air about him, a self-appointed distance. 'Useta think about putting in air-conditioning.' He wiped his long upper lip. 'That was before your friend Goof took charge of course.' He had assumed from the start where our sympathies would lie. 'I tell you what, everyone's gunna feel the pinch this Christmas. All your university types, your bra-burners, unionists and what have you. They aren't gunna like it any more than we do.'

He waved his hand at us, our bare feet, the ragged deckchairs, the cockeyed flywire door. Which side did he put us on now? We sagged back. Once I had taken him on, look there's a world recession, think what's been done for the etc, but I'd lost energy in the end, retreated — well anyway, it all boils down to, maybe it's just a temperamental, it's not that I'm really into . . . (Wes, where are you? . . .)

'I hope he doesn't stay long', Angela said in the kitchen. She was trying to light her little camper stove to make a cup of tea. 'He'll wake up Nat the way he carries on.'

'I hate it when we all just sit and take it', I said. 'Pod's pet hippies.' I muttered like this sometimes to Angela, when we were alone. Angela never seemed to hear. She was always doing something, providing something. I hovered behind her with the vague reflex feeling that I ought 'to help'. I tried to wash out some cups in the sink but it was full of drowning nappies.

There was a cough from the bedroom, and a long surprised wail.

'There!' said Angela. She paused on her way out. 'It's all Gough's fault of course.'

I was left, free to prowl. Since Poddy had come, you could disappear behind that beaded curtain in the country, 'women's work'. You only had to turn up with the tea. The flame beneath the kettle flickered near to extinction. Angela must be running out of gas.

Angela's kitchen was a lean-to, tacked onto the back wall of the cottage. The city owners asked no rent on the understanding that Vic would build a proper kitchen. He had laid the concrete slab for the floor. The dark end of the room still held the cement-mixer and a jumble of tools. Into the weatherboard wall, between the louvres, Angela had knocked a dartboard of nails. Here hung her pots, her mugs and nappy-pins, her dusty bunches of drying rosemary and everlastings. Postcards from friends in New Zealand and Bali and Nepal were wedged in between the boards.

From the doorway I could see onto the verandah. Vic now held his son, loosely, high up on his chest, his dark face blank as if to say 'this makes no difference to me'. Poddy was still talking. I thought how people in middle-age seemed to occupy their own features, they seemed over-drawn, stamped with use. Like babies, they were a different species.

I remembered how my own parents used to entertain on summer evenings. They called it 'having a few couples over'. For this my mother would sweep the porch and sponge down the leaves of her pot-plants, wearing a snail curl criss-crossed with bobby pins over each cheek. She would put out guest towels and at the last moment, as the bell rang, shed her shorts and tread into a skirt. Fussed. For a handful of heads on a lit porch — sniper-like my sister and I knelt and picked out favourites — the anecdotal growl of the men's voices, some woman's helpless nervous trill like punctuation, echoing out into the suburb. The vast starry night was undisturbed.

It was in the kitchen, if you padded out in your shortie pajamas, where the women got the supper, heads bent over the hissing kettle, that the evening's true exchange seemed to be taking place.

Were we after all so very different?

And, spying like this, would I have picked out Wes to like, to watch, *mine,* as he yawned, as his bare satiny shoulders curved guard again over his guitar?

The first thing we had done when we came to the farmhouse was to set up the stereo on its packing-case frame in the empty living-room. At last, full volume. The wet paddocks, the stolid hill received Zappa, Jeff Beck, the Allman Brothers. This was the environment we were used to.

'10, 9, 8, 7, 6 . . .', shouted Pod on our doorstep one knife-cold night. 'When the hell is blast-off?'

Wes started putting on more and more country blues. Even if we were talking, after a while Wes's eyes slid sideways as his head chased up a beat. Those nostalgic voices were stronger than our own. In the mornings I would know that he had gone by the absence of music. These days he was leaving earlier and earlier for the garage.

I could not train myself to become a morning person. I had counted on this just happening in the country. Change of regime = change of person. Was this part of my work-ethic upbringing or was it really profoundly Zen? Funny how much they all seemed to be linking up; Bad Karma = Reap as Ye Shall Sow etc . . . I lay on the mattress on the floor and tried to think about this. The sun slanted in through the broken venetian blinds.

The Inner Light grows in Silence and Concentration. I had to shut my eyes not to read this on the sun-slashed wall, not to see myself, felt pen in hand, on our first night here. My own uneven letters mocked me like graffiti. Yet still I did not try to remove them, or even cover them up.

In the city, in the big house where I had met Wes, the walls carried signs like a political meeting place. Indian gods behind the kitchen door. Over the stove, a newspaper cutting of Whitlam and Barnard waving after they had announced the conscription amnesty. A big mandala above the fireplace in what had come to be called the meditation room.

I'd thought then it would be easier to meditate in the country, to get up, work in the vegetable garden . . .

The vegetable garden was no more. Such as it was, some lettuce-pale silver beet coiled up like flags and other, unidentified fronds, had disappeared entirely one weekend when we were in Perth. Tours of inspection now included not only the pen where we *could* have chooks, but the vegetable garden's graveyard, its frail wire netting looping among the grass, its scarecrow climbing canes.

Anyway, why were vegetables such an index of virtue? The eating of them, their growing, the disposal of them back to the earth?

. . . *In Silence and Concentration* . . . The 'S' was oversize, it seemed to leer at me . . .

The house was not silent. It was a hollow contained within a sleeve of animal life. In the ceilings and walls, under the floor, rats, cats, possums were they? skittered and thundered on ceaseless missions. The sleeve had holes. At night they gambolled in the passage ways with the whispery abandon of out-of-hours children. Now the house itself creaked hospitably as its joints expanded in the heat of the sun. Crows bleated out in the paddocks. The day was cranking open before me.

Some time before we came here, this house had been dispossessed of its land and left to perch as a rental proposition on the crossroads between the town and the hill. A previous owner had tried to turn it into a city house, *à la mode*. You cleaned your teeth over a water-buckled vanity bench. The toilet had just made it inside, wedged in, not quite square, home-tiled next to the shower. (While the old dunny lurked outside among the grasses, its round white pedestal crouching in intimate darkness, its door forever on the point of being closed.)

A breakfast bar butted across the kitchen on spindly legs where a big wooden table should have been. The fireplace had been boarded up. On the sink a single cup trailed the tail of a tea-bag. The guitar sat in the one comfortable chair.

There was only the country women's programme on the radio. It was like being home, sick, in the suburbs at midday, part of a community of grandmothers and invalids waiting behind lowered blinds. The heat here islanded you to the shelter of your own roof.

Outside the kitchen window the long yellow grasses marched up from the paddocks, consumed the fences, halted at the edge of the firebreak beside the straight gravel road. Although the day was still they shimmered and rocked, an imported pastoral ideal. I grabbed my shoulder bag and shut the front door behind me with a bang that sent Wes's Javanese wind-chimes into brief, oriental applause.

It seemed quieter out on the road. Just the regular swish-swish of my thongs on gravel, throwing up little ankle wings of dust, and a great airy stillness around me. Crows rose and fell in the distance. The sun swamped everything. The drab homespun belly of the hill was exposed, too close behind me. I walked fast towards the haze over the town. I became an engine pumping up heat. I was haloed an inch over with my own heat. I thought about Coca Cola in thick glass bottles. I thought of shopping centres, as of great humming cathedrals. I thought of pine trees and of wading into the cold oil of the sea on a hot day. Although I had never been to a dinner party, I thought about soft lights and crystal glasses, and the fine picking up of lines of thought. Cheeses and wines, meat in cream, all that refined acid food that made you aggressive and decadent. And interesting. I trod out my own stale band of thoughts, oblivious to the landscape. While my higher mind slumbered, unsummoned for yet another day.

There was always a moment, as Angela and I turned into the main street, that I saw the town as distanced, through a lens, and our approach to it as something slow and heroic, a response to a sudden call for 'Action' . . . The two women trudge on, faces to the sun, their long skirts blowing against their bodies . . . The pusher rattled a pony-cart accompaniment, a flimsy candy-striped city job that jolted poor Nat sideways, his towelling hat across his eyes, his fat fists clenched on either knee.

'Whoa there boy', sang out Angela, swooping down and straightening him, her long hair still damp from the paddling pool where I had found her, balancing Nat on her naked brown stomach. She and Nat smelled of talcum powder.

The main street narrowed down to vanishing point before us as it sped on into the wheat-belt. The shopfronts rose into turrets and mouldings, the clock in the Town Hall struck midday against the white-blue sky. But as we entered the town, past the dusty Municipal rose garden, the wide street swallowed us, and the shops broke into their familiar sequence, the Co-op, McIntyre's Newsagency, 'Verna' Hair Salon, the Post Office, Kevin Scragg's, The Bright Spot.

Why was shopping so consoling? A relief from the daily round of giving out, these small smooth purchases bumping against you, a newspaper, stamps, a bucket and spade for Nat, fresh bread, the first watermelon! It was like nourishment . . . especially with Angela who did not worry about confusing wants and needs, who rummaged and fingered passionately while the Co-op girls, school-leavers with engagement rings, clustered around the pusher. 'Isn't he *gor*-geous!' they cried.

The pusher rolled on, Nat unblinking, wedged among the parcels.

'Just a minute', Angela said, when we had nearly passed the butcher's. 'I've got to get a chop for Vic.' Vic was an unrepentant meat-eater. He added a chop or some polony to Angela's wok vegetables and united them with tomato sauce.

'I'll wait outside with Nat', I said. I did not even like to catch Kevin Scragg's eye as we walked past, his knowing salute, chopper in hand. He liked to ask you how you were finding life in the country, and to read your T-shirt, eyes lingering, for the benefit of the other customers. You knew, by the little silence as you made your way to the door, that you were going to be talked about as soon as the bell rang your exit.

I pushed the legitimising pusher back and forward under the window. At the kerb a girl in high-heeled sandals was stowing groceries and a baby into the back of her car. She gave me a quick church-porch smile across the pavement. Loretta Wells — one of the Wells. Did she see me as a sort of poor-white, a younger version of Mrs Boon, who shuffled in to town with a shopping trolley from out near the drive-in?

Through the window I saw Angela's bangles shiver down her arm as she took her tiny white parcel from Kevin Scragg's outstretched hand. The hand held, for a moment the parcel was a tug-of-war with Angela laughing and shaking her head.

'Let's go', she muttered as she joined me, her escape jangling behind her. 'I'm not going in there if he's on his own again.'

Poddy's garage was a block further down the road. Out in the yard Wes's ute and Vic's Kombi were nosed up next to one another.

'Vic!' called Angela. We stood at the top of the driveway leading down to the black mouth of the workshop. A transistor was playing loudly in its depths. We waited. Vic came out slowly, paused at the door, took out his tobacco.

'Want to come to the Bright Spot with us?'

'Na — got a job on.' He squinted up at us over the paper bandaided across his bottom lip. He clicked his tongue at Nat. I cleared my throat.

'Is Wes about?' I hardly ever spoke to Vic. He wore footy shorts and workman's boots; he propped one shapely leg across the other, leaning on the workshop door. You could glimpse an earring through his tangled hair. 'Wes!' he called out over his shoulder.

Poddy's red beanie shadowed Wes at the entrance. Wes was carrying a coil of rope and the transistor. They were moving towards the yard.

'Any chance of a lift home?' I said.

'No way.' Pod answered for him. 'He's gotta follow me in the truck.' Wes lifted his shoulders above his armful and gave an idiot-grin. He called himself a grease-monkey these days. He marched off, Pod right behind him. With his pony-tail and his big boots he looked like the garage mascot.

'Wait at our place.' Vic gave a nod in the direction of the river. 'Have a sewing circle or something.' He breathed out smoke and smiled broadly at us, conscious that he might have gone too far.

'Do you see yourself living here always?'

'Always?' Angela frowned as if it was a word she didn't know.

I knew it was a low-consciousness sort of question. All because I couldn't bring myself to ask: Are you happy? I drew up hard on my strawberry milkshake. There was a lot of it, it tasted of crushed chewing gum, I felt it flooding through every cell of my body. *Daily renewed sense-yearnings sap your inner peace . . .*

We were sitting at one of the laminex tables in the Bright Spot, the traditional end to our shopping trips. There had been times, when Vic and Wes were with us, playing the pinball machines amongst the town's milling adolescents, that we had recognised the Bright Spot's fly-spotted nostalgic charm. Today we were the only customers. Most of the chairs were stacked on the tables up near the kitchen. A whirring fan bowed to us from the counter.

'Actually', Angela said, 'Vic's talking about moving on. He'd quite like to try opal mining up at Coober Pedy.'

The plastic streamers in the doorway swayed and kicked in a gust of afternoon wind, straight from the desert. A jumpy brightness was suddenly flung across the table.

'Do you want to go?'

'I don't know.' Angela pushed back her fringe and for a moment her small forehead stared out, white, next to her hand. 'I don't mind I guess.' She looked past me towards the door.

We looped our bags over our shoulders and prepared for that moment of darkness through the plastic streamers. There seemed to be a new silence between us as we set off again, into the glare of the long afternoon.

My parents had come to visit Wes and me. This time Evvie, my sister was with them. It seemed crowded in the kitchen round the breakfast bar. Outside the whole country spread, bland in the late afternoon sun. But for all of us the world had shrunk, temporarily, back to this, wary faces across a shadowed table. Between us was the cake-tin with the Highland Tartans border. We ate the cake from it over our crossed knees. Christmas cake, my mother's year-round speciality. Before she left I would give her back the tin, empty. It would come back full again.

Evvie didn't eat the cake. She filled in time examining the kitchen. She was seventeen now; all at once she had very long legs in very tight jeans. Her blouse, satin with little ragged caps of sleeves, was the sort of thing you find by a dedicated haunting of the op-shops. Her blank survey of my kitchen said *Not for me.*

'You've been making jam!', my mother said, smiling.

'Mm. Fig.' She would never know how I had flung the figs, my only crop, into Angela's big pot, bored, martyred, mad with itching . . . 'You can take some home with you if you like.' With any luck my mother would forget. Though out of desperation for some proof of this life-style, fruits at last, she would probably persist in pushing the tarry substance across her morning toast . . .

'Still no job turned up for you?' my mother asked me. 'You'll be getting broody if you hang around too much.' Her laugh turned uncertain. She had to go on. 'I'm too young to be a grandmother!'

My father stirred. His big form was hunched up in one of our frail chairs. I hoped she wouldn't go further. I hoped she wouldn't say: 'Mind you, there's a lot less hypocrisy about the young people of today'. But she turned and looked out the window. 'Oh this poor dry countryside', she said. She sighed.

I knew how to look out that window, to see, defined against her, the grasses moving for a moment across that other landscape, *the country,* luminous in fading light, waiting for us.

'How's the guitar going Wes? Do you get enough time to practise?' My mother had turned to Wes.

Wes looked up. 'Oh I get around to it now and . . . haven't had a really good session for a . . .'
'He's been working really hard at the garage', I said.
My mother smiled at him, nodding. 'It's a wonderful chance to learn a trade.'
Then my father did something surprising. He uncoiled his hand from his elbow where it had seemed to be holding him contained. He stretched it across the table, his red, whorl-jointed hand, part of my former life, and picked up Wes's restless fingers.
'These aren't mechanic's hands', he said. He put Wes's hand down gently. He didn't look at anybody. He cleared his throat in a business-like way.

I was sitting, crease-eyed from a heavy siesta, on the front steps of the farmhouse. From time to time I ducked in through the open front door to put the needle back onto my favourite sides of Wes's records. This was something that I was too shy to do when he was home. I felt I probably liked them for the wrong, unmusical reasons, for the feelings they gave me, their melancholy landscapes: I waited for certain songs, to retaste that sensation of the right chord struck, again and again . . . Bonnie Raitt singing 'Guilty' and 'I Thought I was a Child', Linda Rondstadt's 'I Never Will Marry', Randy Newman's 'Louisiana' . . .

'They're tryin' to wash us away
They're tryin' to wash us away',

I droned, private, flat, stamping empty time on the step below me, calling up something to happen.
The step was still warm from the day, but the glare was gone. Lights began to trace the streets of the town. Dogs barked.
A pair of headlights was advancing up the road with the darkness. I heard the home-coming changing of gears. The ute.
'Did you listen to the news tonight?' Wes called as he came towards me up the path. 'Have you heard?'
'What?'
He stood before me on the steps. 'Gough's been sacked.

Kerr's sacked Whitlam.' He wore the half-smile of the news-bringer.

'When?' I stood up too.

'This morning. It came through about midday. Fraser's forming a government.' He was edging past me up the steps. 'Pod's been at the pub all afternoon', he called on the way down the hall. 'It's pretty wild down there. You'd think they'd won a war or something.'

He came out again with his guitar.

'Where are you going?'

'They want some live music.'

'You're going back there? Now?'

Wes gave a swift loop of the ute keys over his fingers. His eyes flickered. I felt the wordless authority of his feeling, that chose when he came forward, or kept back.

'I'm going to play', he said.

The fire when it came was swift and stealthy.

On a day when the sun hung venomous, whitening, striking sharp light off leaves, I heard a distant crackling like a friendly winter hearth. I looked out the window and saw a low line of flames snake across the paddock as if it rode along a fuse.

From the verandah, down the hill, a truck was crawling up the road, the fire's keeper. I could just make out the figures of some men by the fence, and then they were lost in billowing smoke.

I thought: Do they know I am here?

The fire took over. The house was darkened. I ran from room to room shutting the windows. A roar seemed to run under the roof. I heard the windchimes' futile alarm.

I stood by the kitchen window and watched the flames pass the house in vast erratic tacks across the grass.

For a complete list of books available from Penguin in the United States, write to Dept. DG, Penguin Books, 299 Murray Hill Parkway, East Rutherford, New Jersey 07073.

For a complete list of books available from Penguin in Canada, write to Penguin Books Canada Limited, 2801 John Street, Markham, Ontario L3R 1B4.